CW00501910

ROCKSTARS
DON'T LIKE
SPARKLY THONGS

NIKKI ASHTON

Copyright 2017 by Nikki Ashton
All Rights Reserved ©

ISBN 978-1-7991198-3-8

Rock Stars Don't Like Sparkly Thongs
Published by Bubble Books Ltd

The rights of Nikki Ashton as the Author of the work has been asserted
by her in accordance with the Copyright and Related Rights Act 2000
All rights reserved. No part of this publication may be reproduced,
stored in a retrieval system, or transmitted, in any form or by any means
without prior written permission of the publisher, nor be otherwise
circulated in any form or binding or cover that in which it is published
and without a similar condition being imposed on the subsequent
purchaser. A reviewer may quote brief passages for review purposes
only

This book may not be resold or given away to other people for resale.
Please purchase this book from a recognised retailer. Thank you for
respecting the hard work of this author.

Rock Stars Don't Like Sparkly Thongs
First published in a private group July 2017
All Rights Reserved ©

Cover design – JC Clarke of The Graphic Shed

This book is a work of fiction. Any references to historical event, real
people or real places are used fictitiously. Other names, unless used
with specific permission, characters, places and events are products of
the author's imagination. Any resemblance to actual events, places or
persons living or dead, are entirely coincidental.

ACKNOWLEDGMENTS

♥

This book is for my readers – especially my angels.

You're all amazing and I can't thank you enough for the support that you give to me.

Because of your love of Dirty Riches and I just had to write this for you

Love ya long time

Nikki xx

ROCK STARS CAST OF CHARACTERS

The Men

Luke Mahoney – Lead Singer Dirty Riches
Anthony 'Skins' Ballard – Drummer Dirty Riches
Tom Davies – Bassist Dirty Riches
Jake Hughes – Lead Guitarist Dirty Riches
Noah Hendricks – Luke's nephew and Betty's Husband

The Women

Martha Mahoney – Luke's wife and former housekeeper
Stacey Ballard – Skins wife
Amber Hughes – Jake's wife and Luke's cousin. Former PA
for Dirty Riches
Lucia Mahoney – Luke's mama
Betty Mahoney – Martha's daughter and Luke's step-
daughter
Abbie Davies – Tom's Wife and Jake's half-sister - former
Hollywood actress

The Kids

Ethan Ballard –son of Skins and Stacey
Rocco Mahoney –son of Luke and Martha
Eliza Hughes –daughter of Jake and Amber
Hendrix Hughes – son Jake and Amber
Giovanna 'Gigi' Mahoney – daughter of Luke and Martha
Jackson Ballard – son of Skins and Stacey
Rafa Mahoney – son of Luke and Martha
Hettie Davies –daughter of Tom and Abbie

CHAPTER 1

♥

PRESENT DAY

"Twenty-fucking-years," Tom grumbled, with a shake of his head. "I can't believe we've been going that long."

"There were times I didn't think we'd last twenty more minutes, never mind years." Luke let out a long sigh as his eyes raked over the photographs that were laid out on the desk. "It's actually longer than that, if you count those years schlepping around bars in our crappy van."

It was the 20th anniversary of Dirty Riches being in

the business-signing their first record deal-and Neil, their manager had agreed that 'Rock Anthem Magazine' could do a five-page article, with a centre-spread pull out poster. The band were picking out the photographs for the collage poster, before they took part in a series of group and individual interviews.

"That one has got to go in." Jake stabbed at a photograph of Tom wearing a leopard print bikini.

"Fuck off," Tom growled. "It's bad enough that you made me wear it, but that fact that my balls are hanging out is not good."

Skins looked over his shoulder and burst out laughing. "Shit you've got real hairy nads, dude."

Jake bent over to study the picture, his nose almost touching it. "How can you see he's got hairy nads?"

"If you picked it up you might be able to see. Or maybe if you actually wore your glasses you wouldn't need to."

"Ugh, fuck off." Jake grimaced and shuddered. "I'm not touching *his* hairy nut sack."

"It's not *actually* my nuts, it's a fucking photograph you dick."

"Doesn't matter, I'm not touching it. And for your information, Luke, I do not wear fucking glasses."

"Liar. I saw them in your jacket pocket, so just put the fuckers on."

Jake curled his lip at Luke and chose to ignore him, before turning to look at the rest of the photos. Skins laughed and slapped him around the back of the head.

"You're one vain fucker, you know that."

"Hey Skins," Jake cried, in mock excitement. "You dropped this." He flipped a finger at his band mate and with a huff, picked up a photograph. "Shit, look at this one."

He held up a picture between his thumb and forefinger, laughing to himself as his friends gathered around.

"Oh my god," Tom groaned. "Look at the state of us? How cool did we think we looked?"

The picture was of them all lined up, leaning against a wall, wearing black jeans, white t-shirts and black leather jackets. They were all seventeen years of age and trying to look mean and moody.

"That was the promo picture for our first gig, do you remember?" Skins said, taking the photograph from Jake. That girl from college took it."

"God, yeah," Tom said, nodding. "What the hell was her name?"

"Jenny Parker," Luke muttered.

"Oh yeah." Tom's eyes widened as he turned to Luke, smacking him on the back. "You had sex with her in the college theatre, didn't you? And, if I remember rightly, you gave the A-level drama class a good show."

"Yeah," Jake chipped in. "You were shagging her on stage behind the curtain when they all came in to rehearse the end of year play."

Luke scrubbed a hand down his face and groaned. "Fuck. The drama lecturer pulled the curtain back and there was me, balls deep and my bare arse pumping away."

"You dirty bastard," Skins said with a chuckle.

"I wasn't the only one," Luke protested. "We've all got our fair share of shag tales to tell."

They all thought about it and nodded.

"What if they ask us about them in the interview," Skins said, moving to sit on the couch in their manager's office. "Do we tell the whole truth?"

"Not a fucking chance," Tom replied, shaking his head vehemently. "I like my balls thank you very much. It's one thing for Abbie to know about my past, but for it to be in print for Hettie to see would not be conducive to me having any more kids."

Jake laughed and hooked an arm around Tom's neck. "Hettie isn't even one yet, how the hell can she read it?"

"Not now, but it'll be in print for ever more. It's bound to rear its ugly head when she *can* read it. I'm telling you, if that shit appears in print Abbie will have my balls in a vice and cut them off with a blunt knife."

"Yep, Martha too," Luke agreed. "And I'm betting Stace and Amber will feel the same way."

Skins and Jake looked at each other and nodded.

"So, what do we do if they do ask us?" Tom asked.

"Just say we don't want to discuss it." Luke said, moving to sit next to Skins. "Explain it wouldn't be fair on our wives or kids. There are plenty of other things they can ask us about."

"I don't want to talk about it either, I don't wanna disrespect Freckles," Jake said, referring to his wife by the nickname he gave her. "But at the same time, those experiences are part of us, part of what have kept us tight over the years. We did all that shit and if we don't talk about it will they just dredge up some of those groupies to give their side of the story?"

"Nah, they won't...will they?" Tom asked. "I mean, surely they wouldn't. Neil would just pull the interview."

It was true. Neil Cornelius, their manager, would have no qualms about doing that if it meant protecting his boys. He'd been with them since they'd got their first record deal-and had been appointed by the record company-and had stayed with them, now being employed by Dirty Riches. He'd always been protective of them, steering them in the right direction, and in return they'd respected him and made sure he reaped the benefits of their success. He was now in his early sixties, but still as wily and astute as he'd always been.

"That might stop Rock Anthem publishing that shit, but not other magazines or papers. This interview and the anniversary gig are going to create a lot of interest, so if a paper can ride on its fucking coat tails by dragging up some woman that one of us, or even all of us, has shagged, they will." Luke looked at them all in turn. There'd been one occasion where they'd all indulged in group sex with a couple of women and that was not something he for one, wanted to come out.

"Fuck," Skins groaned. "I do not want Stace finding out about that."

"We were nineteen," Tom protested. "Surely they wouldn't drag that up, would they?"

Luke nodded. "Yeah, I reckon they would, and it's not something I'm particularly proud of."

"I don't know," Jake said, with a grin. "If I remember you gave a sterling performance."

Tom and Skins snorted a laugh, but Luke stared at Jake with narrow eyes.

"Not fucking funny, dicktwat."

"Oh, but it was." Jake laughed and flopped down on to the sofa opposite to that Luke and Skins were on.

"Whatever. We need to agree that we don't talk about it in the interview. We all need to stick together and make sure Neil makes it a stipulation of the interview-no talk about previous sexual exploits."

They all nodded and Tom sighed.

"Yeah, but we did have some fun."

"True, sugar tits," Jake said. "We did."

"Hey," Skins cried, startling them. "Do you remember when-."

CHAPTER 2

♥

18 YEARS EARLIER

As Skins entered the green room, he could feel all eyes of Dirty Riches on him. The room was buzzing with people, music execs, competition winners and some guests of Neil their manager, but the only people watching him were the band. No one else gave a shit where he'd disappeared to with the curvy redhead. Those fuckers though, they'd give him shit. Particularly as he'd had a blow job from a brunette only minutes before they'd gone on stage to do their set. Okay, he thought, he'd take their shit for a few minutes and then politely tell them to fuck off.

"Where've you been?" Luke asked, before taking a bite out a sandwich.

"Bathroom." Skins lowered his eyes to the floor and moved over to the table that was laden with bottles of spirits and beer. "Why is there no damn water on here?"

"What's up, you need to replace some major bodily fluids?" Jake grinned at him, shifting the blonde on his knee. "Shit, careful beautiful, you've kinda got my nuts trapped."

"I can massage them for you," she purred, seductively licking her top lip.

Jake studied her and wondered when was the last time she'd taken her make-up off and replaced it with fresh, rather than slapping more over the top of the old stuff. Not in a while, was his guess.

This was their first proper tour-at least one that wasn't in pubs and saw them arriving in a van and unloading their shit themselves. This tour was supporting the massive rock band Mercy Child and with the tour bus and roadies, came groupies. Three weeks into a twelve-week tour however, and Jake was already getting bored with the same jaded faces that looked up at him while they sucked him off.

"Listen, Sharon-."

"It's Shania, like in 'Twain'," the blonde said, sticking her ample tits out.

"Sorry, Shania. So, listen babe, I think you need to

9

go now. It's been fun but I need to kick back with my boys here." Jake indicated the rest of Dirty Riches with his hand. "You know, give Skins some crap about his dick falling off if he doesn't calm it down-that sorta thing."

"But I can be funny," Shania protested. "I have jokes."

Jake shook his head and gently pushed Shania off his knee onto the dark brown corduroy sofa. A sofa that he was sure if he looked carefully at, he would see the DNA of many rock stars past and present.

"It's not just a case of being funny," he replied, standing up. "I mean look at Tom, he doesn't have one funny bone in his whole body, but we like having him around. Don't we sugar tits?"

Tom rolled his eyes and sighed. "Yeah, fuck face, you do."

"So, you see," Jake continued. "It's more to do with, I don't want you around any longer."

"Shit," Luke groaned. "That was fucking brutal even for you."

Shania stood up and thrust her hands to her hips. "How dare you speak to me like that?"

"Well, probably because you were on your knees with my dick in your mouth, within five minutes of meeting me."

Jake took hold of her arm and turned her towards the door.

"Off you go," he said, giving Shania a gentle push

and slap to her backside. "If you wait for an hour or so, Mercy Child will be finished and I believe Roy the bass player likes his women on their knees."

"You just can't handle me," Shania called over her shoulder. "And for your information your dick isn't as big as you seem to think it is."

"Fucker!" Jake cried, slapping a palm to his chest. "You take that back. You know that's just not true."

Shania didn't answer, but simply flipped him the bird over her shoulder as she sashayed out of the room.

"You're a mean shit, you know that?" Skins shook his head and flopped down onto the sofa.

"Like she earned any respect," Jake replied, joining him. "I know for a fact that she went through two roadies and a sound guy before she got to me. I'm just a mere step up to the big boys. I'm the one that's been disrespected. I'm actually quite hurt that she's used me in such a way."

Jake pouted and flapped a hand up and down in front of his face, pretending to cry. They all burst out laughing, causing a few people to swivel around in their direction.

"So, what's the plan?" Tom asked, as their laughter died down. "We going clubbing or not?"

Luke shrugged. "I suppose we should."

"Why?" Tom asked, taking a swig of his beer.

"Because, sugar tits," Jake replied with a sigh. "We're on our way to being rock stars, so we need to act like them. Going to a club is a rock star thing to do."

"We don't *have* to," Skins said, feeling so bone tired that all he wanted to do was sleep. "Let's be different, let's not be those typical, young rock stars."

"So, what do you suggest? Go back to the hotel and have a game of scrabble?" Luke asked.

"Yeah," Jake cried. "I love scrabble."

Skins gave him a withering look and turned to Luke. "No, I'm not saying that, but we don't have to go to a club. We can have fun other ways."

"Yeah, like what?"

"I don't know, Thomas," he snapped. "Maybe we can go to Neil's room and find out whether that really is a fucking wig he wears."

They all turned to look at their manager, Neil. He was short, perma-tanned and had a thick mass of hair that looked distinctly wig-like. Luke was convinced he'd seen the stitching once.

"Fuck yeah." Jake said, sitting up straighter. "Let's do it. He'll be here for ages."

"And he's taking those execs to dinner." Luke indicated over his shoulder.

Jake's eyes gleamed. "Fucking game on, I say."

"Hang on," Tom said. "I know I'm the stupid one, but what do you expect to find when he's here and wearing the damn thing?"

They all looked aghast at Tom.

"Shit, he does have a brain."

"Ssh," Luke hissed as they all bundled into the lift to go to Neil's floor. "Don't draw attention to ourselves."

"There are four, pissed up, leather clad rock band members in a lift," Skins said. "How the fuck do you propose we don't draw attention to ourselves?"

At that very moment, just as the door started to close, they heard a squeal of excitement as two women walking through the hotel lobby recognised them, something that was happening more and more. Their latest single had got to number nine in the charts and they'd appeared in a couple of music magazines and on kids Saturday morning TV, so word was getting around. This tour was to be Dirty Riches final stepping stone to bigger things. It was working, they were being recognised and crowds were already screaming for more at the end of their support set.

"See what I mean," Skins replied.

"Okay, don't draw any more attention to ourselves. Tom, you sure you got the right key?"

Tom grinned and handed it to Luke. "Yep, he had no idea."

Tom and Jake had joined forces to trick Neil out of his key. While Jake kept Neil occupied with some over the top tale of how he thought he may have caught an STD, Tom slipped his key out of the back pocket of his trousers.

"Good job you'd seen where he put, and that I was so enthralling," Jake groaned. "Tom's got the touch of Grizzly Bear trying to tie a pair of shoe laces."

"I got it, didn't I?" Tom snapped.

"Yeah, but only because I had to pretend to cry to stop Neil turning around. I honestly think you were enjoying feeling his arse a little too much. I know he works out, but if you really want to feel his tight little buns then leave it until we're all in the gym."

"You're such a dick," Tom sniped at his friend.

"Will you two stop acting like a pair of kids?" Luke growled, smacking Jake around the back of the head. "He got the key, so leave him alone, and remember what you've got to do."

Grinning at each other, Tom and Jake mimed zipping up their lips.

"Pathetic," Luke hissed.

"Sorry, Dad."

Jake's beanie hat went flying as Luke once more slapped him around the back of the head.

As they stood outside Neil's room, Luke turned to the others and put a finger to his lips.

"No fucking kidding," Skins whispered. "I was going to knock on the door and tell him what we'd come for."

Luke gave him a look that told Skins to keep quiet. Their lead singer was not amused.

"You sure he takes a sleeping tablet every night?"

Tom asked Jake.

"Told me he's had insomnia for two years. Funny, that's how long he's been managing us-go figure."

Jake shrugged and adjusted his balaclava.

"What the hell do you look like?" Luke asked, as his eyes moved up and down Jake.

He was wearing camouflage trousers, a black wife beater, and a black balaclava, with only his eyes, nose and lips on show. He'd even tied up his shaggy blonde hair.

"It's my camo gear. If he does wake up he won't recognise me."

"No, but he'll think he's being robbed, scream the place down and you'll be arrested, you numb nut." Skins said with the resigned air of someone who wished he'd kept his ideas to himself.

"I'm a fast runner, now let me at him."

"We don't even know if it is a wig," Tom hissed. "And if it is and you get it, what we gonna do with it? 'Cause I for one don't want it in our room."

"Scared you and Jake will get caught with stolen goods?" Skins laughed at Tom's pouty face.

"No. It's because whatever he washes it in smells like a camel's dick."

"Two things, sugar tits," Jake said, throwing an arm around Tom. "If you don't think that thatch of hair on Neil's head is a wig, then you need glasses. Secondly, I know some of your choices of sexual partners have been a little questionable, to say the least, but how the hell do you know what a camel's dick smells like?"

Tom looked deadpan at Jake. "Why don't you fuck off?"

"Shit," Skins groaned. "His comeback lines just get better and better."

"Okay," Luke said with a heavy sigh. "Let's just shut up so Jake can do his stuff."

He pushed past them and carefully put the key into the lock, turning it slowly and heaving a sigh of relief when he heard the click.

"You're up, Jake." Luke slowly pushed open the door and stood aside for Jake. When Jake didn't appear, Luke looked around. "Jake, where the fu-."

Tom tugged at Luke's sleeve and nodded down to the floor. Jake was lying on his stomach, with a small torch in his mouth.

"What are you doing?" Luke kicked at Jake's side.

"I ooing a omano wall. Whas i ook ike?"

"I think he said he's doing a commando crawl. What's it look like?" Tom explained in a whisper.

"For fuck's sake." Luke scrubbed a hand down his face and groaned quietly. "Just get in there."

Jake gave them a thumbs up and crawled inside the room, leaving his band members tempted to run and leave him there.

"I'll fucking kill you," Neil shouted as he chased the band around the green room the next night. "Let me get hold of just one of you, you fucking little bastards."

They were all laughing hysterically throwing the wig between each other, while dodging their irate manager.

"You little fuckers! How the hell did you get hold of it?"

"Now that would be telling," Jake cried, throwing the wig to Skins. "But let's just say, I'm a ninja."

"Give it back now."

"Sorry Neil," Luke said around a laugh. "No can do. We're kind of attached to it now."

"Yeah," Skins added. "And the audience loved it."

Neil stopped running and with nostrils flaring, thrust his hands to his hips.

"I will never forgive you for this."

"Seriously Neil," Tom said. "You look much better without it. And to be honest, why the fuck do you put it on a mannequins head at night? That's just asking for trouble."

"Yeah, scary as shit," Jake added. "I honestly thought you'd chopped someone's head off for pissing you off. I nearly shit my pants."

Neil shook his head, his face red with anger.

"Oh, come on Neil," Jake cajoled. "It was funny."

"Funny? Funny?" he shouted. "What the fucking hell is funny about you dropping your damn pants on stage and having my toupee taped to your dick and asking the audience if there are any barbers in the house. Nothing fucking funny at all."

The boys had to disagree and fell about laughing while Neil, stormed out with his baseball cap pulled firmly down on his head.

CHAPTER 3

♥

PRESENT DAY

Jake wiped his eyes clear of the tears of laughter. "Shit, that was funny. Neil should have thanked us for getting him out of wearing that stupid thing."

"Apparently, Margo had been on at him for ages to ditch it, but he wouldn't." Luke grinned, remembering the level of Neil's anger that night.

"He made us do early mornings in the gym for a week, do you remember?" Tom asked.

"Shit, yeah. Then we finally cracked and all turned up pissed and wearing women's leotards and tights."

Luke looked at Skins and another memory hit him. Not a good memory.

"You weren't just pissed though, buddy. I remember you being high as a fucking kite."

Skins looked solemn and nodded. That had been the first time he'd tried coke. He'd taken a few lines with a couple of roadies and the bassist of Mercy Child. That had been the beginning of Skins, extremely rapid downward spiral of drug abuse, culminating in him collapsing on stage at Glastonbury. An event that had almost finished the band. Seeing paramedics trying to revive his friend had messed with Luke and he'd ended up with crippling stage fright. Dirty Riches had taken a break for a while, and it was only meeting Martha that had helped Luke to confront his demons and thus get the band back together.

"The slippery slope," Skins said in a whisper. "One thing that I do wish I could go back and change."

"No point looking back," Luke retorted, slapping a hand on Skins' back. "You're healthy now, have a beautiful wife and great kids. A lot to be thankful for."

"Yeah, you're right. I just wish things with Stace had been different at the beginning."

"What, the fact that you met her while you were getting your dick sucked by someone else."

Tom shrank back when Skins growled at him. "Not funny Thomas."

"Sorry, man, but you need to laugh and stop letting that stuff fuck with your head. Luke's right, you've so much to be thankful for."

Skins sat back in the armchair that he was in and looked up at the ceiling.

"She put up with so much from me, and we'd only been married a few months when I collapsed. Yet she stuck by me."

"What does that tell you?" Jake asked.

Skins looked up at him, his steel grey eyes narrowed. "That my wife is amazing."

"Yeah she is." Jake stood up and moved back to the photographs on the desk, and flicked through them. "Look at this one, the way she's looking at you."

He held up a photograph that someone had taken of Stacey, watching the band from the side of the stage. Stacey's eyes were firmly on Skins, who was smiling at her. Her hands were clasped together against her chest and it was evident she was in love with the man she was watching.

"That wasn't long after we got together," Skins said, holding his hand out for the photograph.

"When she finally warmed to you." Tom grinned.

"Yeah," Skins sighed, "when she'd warmed to me. You're right, we didn't have the best of starts."

"Shit, she hated you," Jake added. "I remember that night vividly."

CHAPTER 4

♥

13 YEARS EARLIER

Luke studied the tall, dark haired girl hanging around by the food table and wondered where he'd seen her before. She was really familiar. Gorgeous to look at with fine bone structure and long legs in her leather mini skirt, but he definitely hadn't had sex with her. She was far too classy to be a groupie and she hadn't been in any of their videos- because that was what his relationships consisted of these days, a quick blow job with a groupie, or a night with a model or actress from their latest video. He never got to meet 'normal' people or women anymore. Everyone was in the damn industry, or wanted to be in the industry and thought having sex, or being friendly with a member of Dirty Riches would get them where they wanted to be. As he watched the girl for a little longer, he realised that she was alone and looking decidedly uncomfortable. Walking over to her, Luke decided that she really shouldn't be there. Things would get even wilder as the night wore on, and this girl didn't look as though she'd be able to handle it.

"Hey," he said, stopping in front of her. "You okay? You look as though you're lost."

She looked up from her bottle of water, with huge brown eyes.

"No," she sighed. "I'm here with my friend, she knows some guy who knows the band. But, she's disappeared with a guy with blonde hair. He was a bit weird looking to be honest. He didn't have a top on, but was wearing denim shorts and cowboy boots."

Luke laughed. "That'll be Jake. Sorry about that."

"It's not his fault, she's the one that left me on my own. I take it she'll be safe with him though, despite the bizarre dress sense?"

Luke smiled, liking the fact that she had no idea who Jake was, or in fact, who she was talking to.

"Yeah, he's an idiot, but in a good way. He's probably laughing her knickers off as we speak."

The girl shook her head. "Nope, that won't be

necessary. Tina would drop her thong at the promise of a glass of wine-even if it was out of a cardboard carton."

"Ah, okay." Luke looked around the room, there was no sign of Jake so he could have taken Tina anywhere. "Listen, would you like me to arrange a cab for you?"

She inclined her head, her brow furrowing. "You'd do that for me?"

"Yeah, of course, why?"

"Well, I'm guessing you're in the music industry-you know the ripped denims and leather jacket." She waved her hand down Luke's torso." "Don't you normally hit on girls like me?"

"I suppose that would be the usual behaviour of a member of a rock band, but you don't look the sort of girl that would put up with that kind of behaviour. Despite the fact your friend 'Tina' evidently is that sort of girl."

The girl gasped. "Oh shit, you're in the band? I didn't realise, sorry."

"Don't apologise." Luke frowned. "I'm no one special. I just sing for a living."

"I know, but this is your party. I should at least have checked you out before letting Tina drag me here."

"Hey, don't worry about it. At least you're honest."

The girl smiled and Luke realised she really was

too sweet to be around the debauchery of an after-show party.

"Listen, if you go to the back door, Dex, the security guard will get you a cab." Luke pulled out his phone and started to type a text. "I'll let him know you're on the way. How does that sound?"

She nodded and held out her hand. "Thank you, I really appreciate it."

"No problem. I'm Luke by the way."

"Stacey."

"Well nice to have met you Stacey. Maybe we'll see you again sometime, at another show."

Stacey snorted out a laugh. "Doubtful. No offence, but rockers just aren't my thing. My music taste is distinctly less guttural."

That's when it hit him, that's where he knew her from. Stacey, was Stacey Danson the former teenage presenter of 'Sunday Hymns', one of his mama's favourite TV shows. Yep, rockers definitely weren't her thing and she was most definitely at the wrong party.

"Fuck, babe. That's it, take me deeper," Skins groaned, pushing at the back of the head of the girl on her knees in front of him. He thought her name was Melissa, but only because he'd heard her friend call her that before the friend had started to suck face with Tom. Skins hadn't asked for her name, he never did. All he was looking for was gratification to continue the high from his obligatory line of coke when he came off stage-well, he had to admit that had recently gone to two lines of coke and a tequila shot. Nothing else seemed to touch him-give him the buzz he needed to stay standing after a two-hour set.

"Shit, that's good." He pulled in a deep breath and waited as the burn in the pit of his stomach started to grow. "I'm gonna co-."

Just as he was reaching the pinnacle, the door of the room they were in was flung open and he was faced with a very shocked, extremely beautiful girl, with huge eyes and the fucking plumpest lips he'd ever seen outside a cosmetic surgery clinic. He'd had many lips around his cock, and Skins knew natural plumpness when he saw it.

"Fuuuuck," he cried, unable to stop the inevitable, despite their unexpected visitor.

"Oh my God, I'm so sorry." Stacey flung a hand to her mouth and her eyes got wide. She wanted to flee, but was rooted to the spot.

"Shit." Skins groaned, his face contorted as he shot his load into Melissa's mouth.

The girl gave a high-pitched squeak and took a step back. Horror, shock and disgust shadowed her face in rapid succession.

"You wanna join?" Skins asked breathlessly, as Melissa continued to milk him.

As the girl recoiled in horror, Skins immediately regretted the crassness of his words.

"No, I do not!" Stacey cried, distressed. "God, you dirty animal."

Melissa pulled her mouth from Skins dick, with a pop. "What's going on?" she asked, wiping a hand across her mouth.

Ugh, fucking classy, Skins thought, and his hard on wilted quicker than normal after reaching climax.

"I think you should go," he said, holding a hand out to help Melissa up.

"Why? Maybe she should." She nodded towards Stacey in the doorway. "You're in the wrong place, sweetheart."

"Don't worry," Stacey said, her eyes still on Skins. "I'm going."

"Melissa," Skins warned. "Time to go, babe."

"But-"

"Now, Melissa. I'll catch up with you some other time."

Melissa got to her feet and pushed past Stacey, causing her to stumble as she banged her shoulder against Stacey's.

"Hey," Stacey cried, turning to watch Melissa storm down the corridor.

"So, it looks like we're alone," Skins said, shoving his dick back into his jeans and zipping them up. "You sure I can't tempt you to get to know me better?"

Stacey's head whipped around to look at him. Her lip curled and she wrapped her arms tightly around her waist.

"No thank you, as tempting as your absolutely wonderful offer is. I was looking for the exit. Luke told me that Rex or someone would call me a cab." She turned and looked down the empty corridor. "Shit, how the hell did I manage to get lost?"

"I think you mean Dex." Skins laughed. "And, it's easy, these places are like rabbit warrens back stage. Come on, I'll show you the way." As she looked at him, Skins felt his heart miss a beat. Christ, she was beautiful. Her eyes were big, like huge brown pools of melted chocolate and her elegant long, milky skinned neck was just asking to be sucked and marked. He felt his dick start to harden again and he just knew he had to have her. "Although, you could stay and I'll get you a drink and some food."

Stacey's lip curled again, as she looked at him with disdain. "Sorry, but I'd want you to scrub yourself all over in 'Hibiclens' before I'd even shake hands with you, never mind accept a plate of food you'd handled."

Skin's glared at her. "She had her lips around my dick, sweetheart and there's no chance of that coming anywhere near you."

Now he was mad. How dare she accuse him of being unclean? He was a member of the one of the biggest bands in the country, why shouldn't he enjoy the pleasures that came with it. It wasn't as though he didn't wrap his dick when he was inside someone.

He was quite particular when it came to the women he fucked. Groupies could suck his dick, but sex was purely for the women he met who worked in the industry. He and Luke were the same in that respect-Jake and Tom on the other hand, well groupies were their fuck buddies of choice.

"I wouldn't want it to," Stacey retorted, moving her arms over her chest. "You're disgusting."

"I'm a rock star in the prime of my life, why the fuck wouldn't I let a woman to suck me off, if it was what she wanted?"

Stacey screwed up her face and shook her head. "Ugh, I really don't want to know."

"So, I'm supposed to let you judge me without being able to respond, is that it?"

"What response can you give that would possibly make me think any better of you?" Stacey, shifted her bag on her shoulder and looked down the corridor again. "Listen, can you just tell me which way is out and I'll leave you alone so you can call in the next skank."

"They're skanks because they like sex? Shit, you really are judgemental, aren't you?" Skins groaned inwardly. She might be judgemental, but she was hot as hell and her attitude was making him harder by the minute. Shit, he wanted her more now than he had five minutes ago, before she'd opened her condemnatory mouth.

"No, not because they like sex," Stacey said, with a

huff. "But because I'm betting she's already had sex with at least two other people here tonight, and probably has no care about her own safety. Or cleanliness, if the state of her finger nails were anything to go by."

Skins' eyes immediately went to Stacey's neat nails that were painted immaculately in a deep red. Red nails in his experience usually meant they were wild in bed, but then what did he know? She was beautiful, smelled fucking amazing and he was hard as hell for her-but she was a complete bitch.

"You really are a bitch, aren't you?" Skins voiced his thoughts as he moved towards the doorway.

Stacey looked him directly in the eye, not at all scared by the huge, shaven headed man towering over her.

"Not usually, no. I'm quite a nice person, you evidently bring the worst out of me."

"Believe me baby," Skins said in a low tone. "I might bring the worst out of you, but I'd put the fucking best *in* you if you just loosened up a little."

Stacey gasped. "Not a damn chance. No. Never. Not in your life time."

"We'll see baby," Skins chuckled. "We'll see."

CHAPTER 5

♥

PRESENT DAY

Skins sighed and smiled at the memory. "Two months it took me to even persuade her to go on a date with me. I rang her every day, sent text messages every fucking hour and spent hundreds of pounds on getting flowers delivered."

"Thank God her friend Tina, was a big mouth and happy to give up Stace's number and address. Thank God for my magic dick, eh. You'd have never have managed to persuade her." Jake grinned widely and took a sip of his coffee.

"Don't let Freckles hear you say that," Tom replied. "I don't think she'd want to hear about it."

"I'm damn sure she wouldn't," Jake said. "She knows I wasn't a saint. Shit, she was on tour with us for a year, she saw it first-hand. I still don't want to her to hear about it though."

Amber had been the band's PA for a while and just as Stacey had disliked Skins, Amber had detested Jake. It was only when they'd had to share Luke and Martha's house for six weeks, while Jake was incapacitated with a badly sprained ankle that she'd fallen for him.

"You know," Skins said. "After Stace found me with that girl, I never touched anyone else. Not until I had her."

He left out a long breath as thoughts of his beautiful wife caused his heart to jump, and made the pit of his belly fill with warmth. She was his world- her and the boys-and he couldn't imagine a day on this planet without her.

"Did you know straight away?" Tom asked. "You know, that she was the one."

"I knew I wanted her-the minute she opened that damn door. I didn't know I wanted to marry her straight away though."

"When did you realise that? I kinda remember you being all intense and brooding when we were in Europe, but you never actually came out and said she was the one. Not until you told us you'd proposed."

Skins looked at Tom and grinned. "Keep your cards close to your chest, Tom, and only reveal them when you're ready."

"Fastest growing relationship I've ever know," Luke added. "One minute she hated you, the next we're back from the European leg of the tour and a few weeks later you tell us you're getting married."

"Absence, as they say, makes the heart grow fonder. I got back, went to see her and I knew I was in with a chance when she didn't throw me out. She let me sleep in the spare room that night, but I heard her tossing and turning, so I knew then she was as frustrated as I was. I'd been gone for two months with just my hand for company and then she comes into the bedroom, to check I'm okay, wearing nothing but a damn 'Superman' t-shirt and a pair of silky night shorts."

"Hah," Jake cried. "The little fucking minx. She knew exactly what she was doing."

"Yeah," Skins agreed. "She damn well did, especially as she'd put me in the noisiest bed known to man. I tried to throw one out, but it sounded like a damn colony of mice were having a political debate. I swear I heard her giggling at one point."

"You never really left her house after that, did you." Luke stated.

"Nope. Never wanted to. It took me two more days for Stace to let me kiss her, another day to get her clothes off and then two more days after that to get her in my noisy as fuck bed-well her noisy as fuck bed."

"And the rest is a happy history." Tom sighed and pushed up from his seat. "Shit, we are lucky bastards."

"Yeah, we are," Skins agreed. "Me especially. We were only together six months when we got married and in that six months she saw how hooked I was on blow. Yet all she ever tried to do was to help me. Stace could have ended up a widow after just two months. How fucked up is that?" Tears pricked at Skins' eyes, and he didn't care whether he looked a pussy or not. He was ashamed of what he'd put his wife through. "Some ways I'm grateful for that night."

Luke frowned. "You're grateful for nearly fucking dying...shit, you did die. Those paramedics pulled off a damn miracle to get your heart going again."

"Yeah, I know. But if that hadn't happened, I would never have got help. Never gone to rehab, and we wouldn't be here today. Well you guys might have been, but I'd be dead and you'd have some shit, second rate drummer that would never live up to the amazing beats that I'd created over the years." They all smiled, in total agreement with their friend, as he continued. "My boys wouldn't have a dad...fuck, Ethan and Jackson wouldn't have even have been born." Skins' voice cracked as the horror of that thought hit him.

"Yeah, well my friend," Jake said, quietly. "You are here, and we love you."

"Fuck me," Tom groaned. "Jake's getting all sentimental. You're not gonna make us all take up meditation, or yoga or some other shit are you?"

Jake smiled and shook his head. "I'm not responding to you sugar tits. I'm feeling emotional and fuck you."

Luke laughed and scrubbed a hand down his face. "Shit, this reminiscing is hard work, and we've not even been interviewed yet."

"I know," Tom agreed. "I need to sleep. With all these memories and Hettie teething I'm fucking knackered."

"Think of me," Jake said. "I've had three years of interrupted sleep with Hendrix. That kid is a real night owl."

"Karma," Luke said. "For all the shit you've put us through over the years."

"What shit?" Jake exclaimed. "I've been a damn breeze to work with."

"Really, you're being serious?"

"Yes, sugar tits, I really am. You give me one example of when I've caused you shit."

"Fuck me," Luke groaned. "Where do we start?"

CHAPTER 6

♥

13 YEARS EARLIER

As the sun creeped in through the dirty window, Tom wondered whether he would live to see another sunrise. Damn Jake, he was a fucking liability. They'd be lucky if they got out of this alive, never mind with their kneecaps intact.

"I'll kill him," Luke said, shifting in his chair and groaning. "My arms are wrecked."

"Well that's what happens when they're chained behind your back all night," Tom complained. "And don't worry, if you're arms are too weak to maim him, I'll do the job."

Tom and Luke were being held in the basement of a Motorcycle Club, and had spent the night on hard, wooden chairs with their hands and feet bound by chains. Jake had got them into the shit, big time. The only reason Skins wasn't there was because he'd gone back to the hotel to call Stacey, the girl he was hung up on and, also no doubt, to snort shit up his nose.

They were taking a three-day break in Prague, on the European leg of their tour, to film a video, and Luke, Jake and Tom had gone to a bar with a few of the film crew. The bar was on the outskirts of the city and down a side street, and was frequented by a local motorcycle gang. Jake had been the one who'd insisted that they'd gone there-the guy running the food wagon on set had recommended it. They should have realised, seeing as he was covered in tattoos, had gold teeth and had told them his name was Vrah. It was only in conversation with the barmaid, that they'd learned that Vrah was Czech for killer.

Things had started off okay. All of them were slowly getting drunk on 'Staropramen' the local lager. Luke had set up a tab and Jake being Jake, had insisted that they pay for the drinks for the whole bar, including the large group of bikers sitting in a corner. They gladly accepted and invited the Dirty Riches group to join them. The crew sensing danger, said their goodbyes and grabbed a cab back to the hotel. Luke had wanted to go with them, but Jake wouldn't leave the bar, and Tom wouldn't leave Jake. Two hours later and the *'Becherovka'* had been cracked open, and everyone was pretty smashed. Well Tom, Jake and Luke were, the bikers acted as though they'd only been drinking lemonade all night. A group of women had come in, all scantily clad and tattooed, and Jake decided that it was time for the night to take another turn. He picked the girl with the biggest chest, the smallest skirt and longest legs. What he didn't notice was that all the girls were wearing battered leather jackets and had the same raven's head tattoo on their forearms as the group of bikers. Jake grabbed the girl of his choice and pulled her onto his knee and insisted on kissing the life out of her. Within seconds, chaos ensued. A stool was thrown in Jake's direction, missing him by inches. The girl was dragged from his knee and a knife pushed against his throat, while Luke and Tom were held in headlocks by two burly bikers. If they'd been less drunk and a little more attentive, they'd have seen that all the girls had *Dábel Jezdci Vlastnost* on the back of their jackets. This, according to the *helpful* barmaid, who screamed it at them as they were being bundled into the back of van with blacked out windows, said 'Devil Riders Property'- yes, Jake had manhandled a biker's old lady. Said bikers who'd they got drunk with and who all had *Dábel Jezdci* on the back of their leather cuts.

While Luke and Tom had been tied up in the basement, Jake had been dragged off elsewhere. A few punches to the stomach to help him along.

"Shit," Luke hissed. "Do you think they've saved us the bother and *they've* killed him?"

Tom shrugged. "No fucking idea, but I'm sure we'll find out soon. Christ, Luke, how the hell do we get out of this?"

"I don't know buddy. I do know Skins won't be awake yet. We could *all* be dead by the time he surfaces from his nose candy binge. All I know is we could end up eating worms, because of Jake and his fucking need to hook up and get his dick some action."

"Fuuuck." Tom dropped his head, so that his chin rested against his chest. "I've never been so fucking scared in all my life."

Luke didn't answer. What could he say-oh I don't know when I was ten, I went on a rollercoaster at the fun fair and I shit my pants-true, but he wasn't telling Tom, even if it was their last night alive.

They sat in silence, waiting for the dreaded sound of biker's boots on the rough concrete floor. Neither of them had the energy to do anything else. They'd struggled most of the night to try and get free, but the chains were tight and heavy, with more chains tethering their chairs to metal brackets that stuck out of the wall. Escape was hopeless. Even if they'd got free, the door to the basement was thick metal and the only window had bars at it.

"Luke."

"Yeah."

"I love you, dude. I just wanted you to know that." Tom's voice faltered as he looked over at Luke who was on the opposite side of the room. "You've been the one that got us to the top, you know that. You were the one who kept pushing us, and I'm truly grateful for that."

"No, Tom. We were all responsible. We're like a jigsaw and if just one of those pieces had been missing the picture wouldn't be complete. And you," Luke paused and drew in a breath. "And you, you keep us together more than anyone. When we piss each other off you're the one that makes us see that we love each other like brothers. You do or say something that makes us laugh and we forget what we've been arguing about. So, if anyone has kept us together, it's you."

Tom sniffed.

"Don't you fucking cry on me," Luke hissed. "Say something stupid, please buddy. I do not want to go from this mortal coil with you weeping like a girl. I want to go laughing at your fucking stupidity."

"Fuck you, moron."

They both started to laugh, only to be halted by the sound of bolts being slid open and then a key turning in a lock.

"I love you Tom."

"Right back at ya, Luke."

As their chains clanked from their nervous shaking,

the door was pushed open.

"Hey guys, you ready?" Jake grinned at them as he rubbed at his chest and yawned. "Time to go back to the hotel."

Luke's eyes widened and Tom let out a loud growl.

"What the fuck is going on, Jake?" he asked through gritted teeth.

"What I said, sugar tits. It's time to go."

Jake moved towards Luke and unlocked the padlock at his hands and then his feet. As Luke shook the chains to the floor, Jake went to do the same for Tom.

"You better have a good explanation for all this," Luke said, rubbing at his wrists. "How come you're still walking and talking. Why haven't they gutted you and fed you to the fucking birds?"

"What, you'd rather they had? Luciano, you disappoint me."

"Jake, you better start talking now," Tom snapped, pushing up from the chair and rubbing his backside. "Luke's right. How are you still in one piece?"

"Ah that my friend is a long story." Jake scratched at his neck and sighed.

"Hang on a minute." Luke pulled Jakes hand away and peered at his neck. "That fucking hickie wasn't there last night. Who gave it to you?"

"Fuck," Tom cried. "Did you have to be their bitch for the night? Has the whole damn club gone through you? Was that your punishment?"

"Ugh, no. Shit, your imagination is weird."

"So," Luke prompted.

Jake gave them a sheepish grin and moved towards the open door. "Now remember that you love me right. And I bet you've been worried about me, wondering whether they'd killed me, right?"

"What the fuck did you do Jake?" Luke's tone was low and menacing.

"I mean you did set me up with that lady boy when we were in Thailand, don't forget that. And if I hadn't copped a feel in the lift on the way up to my room, things could have turned out very different."

"Jake." Tom took a menacing step towards him. Jake took another step closer to the door.

"I will fucking kill you if this was all some sick joke." Luke's nostrils flared as he drew level with Tom.

Jake grinned and started for the door. "April Fool."

"You little cu-."

The motorcycle gang, it turned out, were a bunch of actors found by Lubor, aka Vrah, and paid for by Jake, who also slipped the barmaid eight thousand Koruna to make it all look real. While Luke and Tom had spent a fearful, uncomfortable night in the cold basement, Jake had made merry with two of the actresses, upstairs in the luxury farmhouse that he'd rented for his plan.

While Jake had found it hilarious, Tom and Luke

had not. Once they caught up with him, they made him see the error of his ways. They didn't touch his hands, they were his livelihood after all. Plus, they didn't have time to rehearse a stand-in. He did have to wear sunglasses for the next couple of weeks, though and for the rest of the tour he had to wait in petrified nervousness, wondering how they were going to get him back.

CHAPTER 7

♥

PRESENT DAY

As Luke let himself into the house, the sound of laughter filled his ears. He smiled and paused to listen. Someone was making Gigi giggle and he had a suspicion it was her big brother, Rocco. That boy, while serious at times, usually about his clothes and hair, had the devil in him too. He loved to make people laugh, and had a whole host of impressions that he liked to use - Jake being his best one. Also, at only eight-years-old, he was already showing signs of being a ladies' man. Recently, he'd come home from school with eleven Valentine's cards that he nonchalantly, put up on a shelf in his bedroom. When Luke had asked him about them, Rocco had merely shrugged and said, 'there were four girls who didn't send me one, which is disappointing'. Yep, Luke knew that his eldest son would no doubt cause him a few grey hairs in the future.

Where Rocco liked to argue and push the boundaries, Gigi and Rafa on the other hand were totally different. When they were asked to do something it was done immediately, even Rafa at almost two knew when to behave. Gigi was very studious and always had her head in a story book or watching nature programmes on TV and she was like a mother hen with the boys. Always comforting Rafa, or chastising anyone who upset Rocco-she was just like Martha, kind and loving.

All three of his kids were different, but they were good kids and he adored them and he would adore their newest arrival too. Martha was six months pregnant with their fourth and final child-something that Luke had been adamant about. It was Martha's fifth pregnancy, and even though she was fit and healthy, he didn't want her to put her body through it again. Alessandra, or Lessie as Rocco had nicknamed her-he was always allowed to nickname his siblings-was a total surprise. They'd talked about maybe having another baby, but the conversation had never reached the serious planning stage. Then, before it did, Martha started to feel sick in a morning and all planning went out of the window. Four kids under the age of ten, and a daughter in her twenties was enough for any couple.

As Luke walked into the lounge, a chorus of 'Papa' greeted him from the children, all playing on the floor. He kissed their cheeks, earning a huge smile from each in return.

"Hey, babe," Martha said, also smiling up at him. "Had a good day?"

Luke stooped down to kiss her mouth, and then her rounded belly. "Yeah, not bad. How you feeling?"

"Fine, Amber took the kids for me so I had a nap this afternoon."

"That's good. Were you good for Auntie Amber?" he asked his children.

"Yep," Rocco replied. "We played hide and seek and Hendrix was hiding and he fell asleep."

"Yeah, an' Auntie Amber couldn't find him an' she was wowwwied," Gigi announced, without taking a breath and not sounding her 'r's' – the same speech impediment that Rocco had once had.

"I bet she was," Luke replied. "'Cause that means he won't sleep tonight."

"Poor Amber," Martha added. "She tries everything to keep him awake in the day. I bet she could have cried."

Hendrix was not a good sleeper at night, so Amber

rarely let him nap in the afternoon, hoping that by bedtime he'd be knocked out.

"She didn't cry, Mummy," Rocco said, sagely. "She cursed a bit, but I pretended that I hadn't heard."

Luke looked down at Rocco with pride and patted his head-but not too hard because messing up the hair would earn him a hard stare. "Good boy."

"Yes, I was Papa." He gazed up at his father, adoration shining in his eyes. "Even though Hendrix was a bugger, I was good."

Luke's head spun to Martha, who was giving him her death stare.

"What have I told you?" she hissed.

"Hey, it's not me," Luke argued.

"Well it's not me he gets it from, so stop swearing in front of him."

"Did Wocco say a wude word?" Gigi asked.

Luke shook his head, as he stooped down to pick up Rafa, who had started to grizzle. "Yes Princess, it's a word we don't use-isn't it Rocco?" He stared pointedly at Rocco, who smiled back and shrugged.

"Rocco." Martha warned.

Luke tried not to smile. He knew he shouldn't but he loved Rocco's spirit. Okay, some would say he was downright naughty, but Luke knew it was just his son testing the boundaries. He was well behaved and extremely well-mannered the majority of the time, and particularly outside the house in front of other people, so Luke could cope with the odd

47

display of rebelliousness within their own four walls.

"Sorry, Mummy," Rocco whispered, knowing by his mother's face that he was on a final warning.

"Okay," Martha sighed. "Now go upstairs and see if Nonna would like a cup of tea."

Rocco scrambled to his feet, with Gigi following him.

"I come too," she cried, chasing after him through the door.

"He's a little terror," Martha said around a laugh, taking a wriggling Rafa from Luke.

"Ah, he's just trying to push our buttons. He's a good kid really."

Martha grinned and shook her head. "You big softy."

As Rafa snuggled against Martha's chest, sticking a thumb into his mouth, Luke watched them and a huge wave of contentment swept over him. He had no idea what he'd done to deserve his life, his woman, but whatever it was he was more than thankful.

"So, have you decided on the pictures for the article?" Martha asked, shifting in her seat to get herself and Rafa comfy.

"Some. There's so many, it's hard to decide. We're separating them into years and then picking half a dozen from each. We're up to our eighth year, so far."

"I bet it's been great to reminisce."

Luke sat down on the sofa next to Martha, and pondered what she said. "Some of it's been good- some not so much. We've talked a lot about Skins' drug problem today, which was hard."

Martha reached out a hand and cupped his cheek. "Babe, it's over now. He's clean and healthy and has been for a long time."

"I know," Luke breathed out. "But it was a fu- flipping crap time."

Martha laughed softly as Luke checked his cursing, even though Rafa was fast asleep in her arms.

"I'm betting you've had a great laugh too."

Luke nodded. "Yeah, usually at Jake's antics. Actually, it's been good. I still can't believe it's twenty years."

"Ah well you're the old men of rock now." Martha poked at his arm.

"Hey, you be careful who you're calling old. I can still show the youngsters a thing or two."

"Oh God babe, I know you can." Martha said breathily.

He was still her Sex God of Rock, no matter what age he was or how long he'd been in the business. Their relationship was good and strong, and a large part of that was their more than healthy sex life.

Luke leaned closer and gave Martha a long lingering kiss.

"I love you," he whispered.

"I love you too." She kissed him back, only

stopping when Rafa stirred. "So, what's your favourite memory been of today?"

Luke lay his head back against the sofa and considered her question. "Hmm, that's difficult. Over twenty odd years we've had some great moments."

"There must be one that stands out."

Luke smiled and tried to hold back the emotion pricking at his throat.

"Oh yeah, there is one…"

CHAPTER 8

♥

20 YEARS EARLIER

As the taxi drove away, Luke couldn't help the huge grin that spread across the width of his face. They'd done it. They'd only gone and signed a record deal and got themselves a real, manager-someone who knew the music business inside and out. Admittedly, the guy needed to do something with his hair, and tone down the tanning bed use, but Luke could already sense that Neil Cornelius was going to be good for them. He hadn't liked their name-one thing he didn't have a clue about-and he had tried to get them to change it, but they'd all been adamant, Dirty Riches was staying.

Walking up the path to his parents' semi-detached home, Luke thought about buying them something bigger. Maybe he was jumping the gun a little, but he could already taste the success. They were going to make it big, he knew it. Luke felt it in his gut. This was the beginning of everything.

They'd played in local pubs and clubs when they first got together, a little over two years ago when they'd first met at college as fresh-faced sixteen-year-olds. Luke had to admit they were pretty crap then, barely able to hold a tune. Individually they were hugely talented, just hopeless as a unit. Luke, however, had been a hard task master, insisting on nightly rehearsals until he was confident enough they wouldn't make themselves look idiots in front of a crowd. Their first gig had been at a college disco, and while they weren't going to win any Brit or MTV Awards, they sounded okay. Plus, the girls were fucking hot for them. While none of them were virgins, by the end of that term each member of Dirty Riches was distinctly much more advanced in their sexual experience.

After the college disco, Luke managed to secure them gigs in pubs and clubs- they'd even bought a second-hand van, or at least Skins' dad had loaned them the money for it. After almost eighteen months of pubs and clubs, Jake saw an advert for a Battle of the Bands contest in Birmingham. The prize money wasn't great, but Luke thought the exposure would be good, so they entered. They didn't win, but the talent scout from Leopard Print Records saw their potential and the fact that the girls were hungry for them-he'd made it pretty clear that night, that Dirty Riches were exactly the sort of band Leopard Print were looking for. Here they were, two months later and Luke and his three best friends, were shaking hands with Neil and signing for a three album deal.

"Luciano, is that you?" his mamma's gentle voice called from the lounge.

"Yeah, Mamma." Luke opened the door and stepped into the cosy room, lit only by the lamp next to the TV. "You're both up late."

He smiled at his beautiful mamma, who still looked elegant, even in a pink fluffy dressing gown. He patted his papa's thatch of black hair that had a few strands of silver running through it.

"We waited for you son," Seamus Mahoney replied, in his soft Irish lilt. "So?"

Luke shrugged, feigning nonchalance, despite the huge scream of excitement that was bubbling inside him.

"They didn't want you?" Lucia, his mother, asked.

Seamus stood up and patted Luke's shoulder. "Their loss son."

Luke couldn't hold it in any longer and pulled his papa to him. "We did it Papa. We signed."

Lucia squealed, while Seamus let out a muffled roar of approval.

"Oh, my goodness." Lucia wrapped her arms around her son and husband. "We're so proud of you."

"Where's Gabby?" Luke asked, pulling free from their embraces. "We need to celebrate."

Lucia rushed towards the door. "I'll go and get her, she's been studying."

As his mother left the room, Luke turned to his father. "Everything is going to change Papa."

"I know, son," Seamus replied, watching Luke with soft eyes. "Some of it won't be for the best either. There'll be hard times and bad times that go along with those good ones."

"Shit, Papa. Way to bring the atmosphere down," Luke joked, playfully punching his papa's shoulder.

Seamus' face hardened. "I'm being serious, Luke. This isn't going to be one long ride of pleasure without any waves along the way. Just remember there's still a lot more work to do. This is only the beginning,"

"I know that," Luke replied, furrowing his brow. Seamus was normally so positive and confident, and Luke couldn't understand why he was being negative. This was a night to be happy.

"I hope you do son, and I hope you never forget that you're no-one special. You're just a lad who can hold a tune, with a bunch of mates who can play instruments at a decent level."

"Yeah, I know that too." Luke was beginning to wish his parents had gone to bed and not waited up for his news.

Seamus had wanted to go with him, make sure everything was above board, but Luke had insisted that it was just him and the guys, and their solicitor. He wanted to prove to his papa that he could do this- do something good for a change, something that didn't bring his parents a headache. After all, his school career hadn't been particularly glowing. Seamus and Lucia had been called to see the Head at least three times a year about Luke's lack of commitment, his bunking off, or some other misdemeanour. Now was his time to do something positive, to make them proud. Or at least that's what he'd hoped-seemingly Seamus didn't quite see it that way.

Seamus placed two large hands on Luke's shoulders and looked intently into his son's eyes.

"I'm prouder you than I know how to express, son," he said, gently shaking him. "I know you'll work hard and try to be the best band you can be- that's your nature when it's something you love. Just don't ever forget where you came from and who you are- that's all I'm saying."

Luke's shoulders sagged as the tension left his body, and he smiled warmly. "I won't, Papa. I promise."

"That's good, because you're a damn fine man and I would hate for people not to see that."

Luke felt the emotion build into a lump in his throat as Seamus took a deep breath.

"I've not done much with my life, Luciano. Not achieved an awful lot, except marry the most beautiful woman in the world and have two amazing children. That to me is more than I ever thought possible for a poorly educated man from a tiny Irish village. But, the moment I met your mamma on your grandpa's vineyard, that was when my life got better. That was when *I* achieved *my* dreams. You though son, you can achieve greatness and you *will* achieve greatness. I know, I feel it here-." Seamus thumped at his chest with the palm of his hand. "All I ask is that you never let yourself down."

Luke swallowed and nodded. "I won't, I promise."

Seamus smiled and pulled Luke against his chest, wrapping strong arms around him and holding him tight. He needed this with his son-needed to hold him tight, because Luke was right, things were going to change.

"I love you, son."

Luke inhaled sharply. He knew his papa loved him and Gabby, it was obvious, but he rarely said it. His mamma did, but not his papa.

"I love you too, Papa."

"Good." Seamus slapped his back and pulled away. "Now, let's crack that champagne open."

CHAPTER 9

♥

PRESENT DAY

Luke laid his head back against the sofa and sighed, as he felt Martha squeeze his hand.

"The next time he told me he loved me, was just before he died," he said, turning to look at his wife. "We were going through shit with Skins, and he found me in the room I used when I was staying with them at their bungalow. I was crying because I had no idea how we were going to save Skins. My best friend was wasting away in front of my eyes and I couldn't do anything about it."

"Oh, babe," Martha whispered, moving closer to Luke, with a sleeping Rafa still in her arms. "It must have been awful."

"Yeah, it was." Luke gave her a soft smile, and stooped to kiss Rafa's forehead. "But Papa came in and just held me, let me cry it all out. Then when I'd finished, he said he was prouder of me at that moment than he'd ever been. Said it was because I wasn't crying about the band, and what might happen to it, but because I loved my friend. Then as I wiped my eyes, he kissed the top of my head and said in that soft Irish voice of his, '*I love you son, more than you will ever know.*' He was dead a week later."

Martha sniffed beside him, and swiped at her tears. "Oh Luke."

"Hey, don't get upset." Luke shifted in his seat, moving so he could put his arms around her. "It's fine, please don't cry."

"I wish I could have met him."

Luke brushed, Martha's long, plumb coloured hair away from her face, before dropping a soft kiss to her trembling lips. "He would have loved you."

"I hope so."

"No doubt, baby. No doubt at all."

As they looked at each other, Rafa stirred, pushing his chubby little arms out and rubbing his face against Martha's t-shirt.

"Hey little man," Luke cooed, taking his son from Martha's arms. "You had a nice little forty winks?"

"Pa-pa." Rafa's face broke into a sleepy smile as he pulled at Luke's ear.

Martha brushed a hand over Rafa's soft curls and leaned to kiss Luke's cheek. "You want a drink?" she asked.

"I'll get it, you rest." With his son in his arms, Luke pushed up from the sofa. "Come on little man, let's go and make mummy and Nonna a cup of tea shall we."

"No-no," Rafa gurgled, waving his arms around.

"Yes, that's right, Nonna." Luke took a deep breath, inhaling his son's scent. "In fact, I think I hear her coming now."

At that moment, Lucia came into the room, holding hands with Rocco and Gigi.

"Hey Mamma," Luke said. "You ready for a cup of tea?"

"Oh, thank you, that would be lovely. How did today go?" she asked, taking a seat in the chair opposite to Martha.

"It was good," Luke replied, shifting a wriggling Rafa in his arms. "Was just telling Martha about it. How difficult remembering some of the stuff was."

Lucia's face softened. "Anthony?" she asked, calling Skins by his proper name, as she always did.

Luke nodded, bending to put Rafa down onto the floor where Rocco and Gigi were now sitting, playing with some cars.

"Yeah, it was a difficult time, but we've had a few

laughs today too. Mostly at Jake."

Martha and Lucia both laughed.

"Oh, you must tell us, over a cup of tea," Lucia said. "Your Jake stories are always my favourite."

Luke laughed and after kissing his mamma's cheek, went out to make the two most important women in his life a cup of tea – oh the life of a rock star!

CHAPTER 10
♥

PRESENT DAY

As Tom pushed through the door of their record company offices, he couldn't help but shake his head in amazement. Musica Records had originally belonged to Luke, but when it started to get bigger, producing top artists and creating numerous number one albums, he'd asked the rest of them if they wanted to buy shares-so for the last three years they'd all owned a part of it. For Tom, it seemed a million years ago that they'd originally signed with Leopard Print. It still amazed him they were making music at their very own record company. A lot had changed in twenty years.

The offices were opened when all the band had settled within a couple of miles of each other. They didn't want to have to go into London, where the main office was, so along with an off-shoot studio, the Manchester base had been created. It was where Neil and some other execs were also based, everyone else working from the London studio. Also, because of both the studio and the one at Luke's house, it meant that the band didn't have to spend days away from home when making a new record.

Tom threw a wave and a wink at Claudia on reception and moved down the corridor to the boardroom where they were going to continue to work through the photographs. The reporter from Rock Anthem was also going to be coming in to have a pre-interview chat, and to talk about what direction the interview would take.

"Morning," he greeted Luke, who was the only one there.

"Hey," Luke replied, flashing him a grin. "I've just sent out for coffee and cake."

Tom glanced at his watch. "It's only just gone ten, haven't you had breakfast yet?"

"Yeah at five this morning. Martha couldn't sleep, the baby was moving around a lot, so we got up and had breakfast."

"You seem pretty perky for being up since five."

"Actually, it was pretty nice to have some us time, you know. No kids interrupting, or shoving fingers in my cereal. I got time with my wife, just to chat." Luke smiled and it lit up his whole face.

"You're not helping to persuade me that more kids is a good idea," Tom groaned.

"Abbie still talking about that?"

"Yep. She doesn't want to have too big a gap between Hettie and the next one, and as Hettie is coming up to one…well she wants to start soon."

Luke waved a hand at Tom. "You'll be fine. I wouldn't swap mine for anything. Yeah, having some time alone is the best thing ever, and it doesn't help that Martha won't employ any help, but the thought of not having the little horrors guts me."

"I guess we just need to make time for us," Tom mused.

Luke slapped his back. "That's about right buddy. Then again, that's how I ended up with another baby on the way."

"So, you going to get the op after this one?"

Tom let out a belly laugh as Luke instinctively felt for his crotch. They'd had this conversation once before, a few years earlier, when Luke was trying to protect Martha from any more difficult births. It had been Tom who'd suggested an elective caesarean, should there be any further Mahoney babies.

"Yep," Luke sighed. "I'm going to get it done in a couple of months."

"So that's the end of the Mahoney offspring?"

"I think so, let's face it we're not getting any younger. I know *I* couldn't go through many more sleepless nights, never mind Martha-she's the one that puts all the hard work in."

"You see," Tom cried, throwing his hands into the air. "Another reason why we shouldn't have any more kids. The sleepless nights."

Luke got up from his seat and leaned over the photographs on the long boardroom table, studying them while he spoke.

"Well maybe you need to get on with it, while we're still fairly young. You don't want to leave it and be going through it again when we're fifty."

"We are nowhere near fucking fifty!" Tom's eyes were wide as he stared at Luke. "Take that back."

Luke turned and gave him a head shake. "Tom, whether you like it or not, we've only got a few more years to go before we reach that fucking number. We're in our forties dude."

Tom grimaced and scrubbed a hand down his face. He did not want to think about it.

"My mum and dad wore cardigans when they were fifty," he said.

"Hah," Luke laughed. "I remember your dad celebrating his fiftieth. We were doing a gig at that club in Manchester, the one where the woman on the door punched Jake and gave him a black eye."

Tom grinned as the memories flooded back. "Oh

yeah, and I was late because I'd had to go out for tea with my folks first."

"Yeah and they dropped you off, and came in without you knowing. Didn't some guy feel your mum up thinking she was into kinky stuff 'cause she was wearing an anorak?"

"Oh fuck, yeah. That was the night they told me I had to leave the band, and get a proper job-in fact they still say that now, twenty-five years later."

Luke smiled warmly at his friend. "Yeah well thank fuck you didn't. We wouldn't be the same without you."

As the two men contemplated that statement, the door flung open and Jake and Skins walked in. Jake was carrying a paper bag and a tray of take-out coffee.

"I just got these from that little nerdy kid that works here-Jeremiah, or something like that."

"Jerome," Luke sighed. "And he's the intern, not the nerdy kid."

"Whatever. He said you'd sent out for them, so I offered to bring them in."

"Where've you two been anyway?" Tom asked. "I thought you were coming in with Luke."

"Luke wanted to get here early," Skins said, taking a coffee from Jake, "had to go jewellery shopping for Martha's birthday, and wanted to be in town at the ass crack of dawn. More to the point, where've you been? Why didn't you come in with us?"

"Oh, Abbie had a dentist appointment this morning, so I stayed home with Hettie. Wasn't sure what time you were coming in. Plus, I had some ironing to do."

"What the fuck!" Jake cried. "Ironing? What the hell has my sister done to you?"

"She puts creases down the front of my jeans, so I do them," Tom replied.

"No way. Shit, I hate that. I just put mine in the tumble dryer, give them a quick shake and they're fine," Jake said. "You should try it."

"Yeah me too," Luke added.

"Have you heard us?" Skins said on a laugh. "We couldn't sound any less like a rock band if we tried."

"It's good though," Jake replied, passing the other coffees around. "I love my life. Don't get me wrong the early days were fucking amazing, but this, now. Well this is the best ever."

Jake was more than thankful for his family. He'd had a deadbeat father, and a mother who was so ill with depression, Jake had been her carer for most of his childhood. For a long time, Dirty Riches were his only family, until Amber came along and rocked his world. Plus, after his dad died, he'd found out about Abbie, his half-sister. Jake finally had the family he'd always wanted, and for him it was better than any music award.

"You don't ever wish you hadn't done it though, do you?" Luke asked, taking a pastry from the paper bag.

"Shit no." Jake shook his head. "We were meant to meet and be in the best rock band on the planet. Otherwise, none of us would have our families and the amazing lives we have now. You wouldn't have bought the big fuck off house next to Martha's cottage. Skins wouldn't have been in a room getting his dick sucked when Stacey got lost. I would never have met Freckles, if I hadn't met you, and sugar tits would never have met my sister-fuck, I probably would never have met my sister. So, no I don't wish I hadn't done any of it. We fucked up a lot, we had a ton of fun and we made a mark on the music world-and still ended up sane and happy."

"Shit, Jake," Tom groaned. "I feel a bit emotional dude."

"Don't cry sugar tits," Jake said, putting an arm around his friend. "I should be the one crying."

"How do you figure that out," Skins asked distractedly as he took his turn to choose a pastry from the bag.

"Because Tom has impregnated my sister. Which means they've done the nasty, and I just can't think about that without being sick in my mouth."

Tom elbowed him hard in the ribs, causing Jake to let out a long breath.

"Fuck that hurt."

"Good it was meant to. Your sister loves me, and we made a fucking beautiful baby, so stop being a knob."

Jake laughed and ruffled Tom's hair. "I love you too, you pillock. I'm just pulling your dick to see if I can get your balls to ring."

Luke sighed and rolled his eyes, amused at the antics of Dumb and Dumber, as he and Skins liked to call them.

"Come on," he said, pulling a chair out from under the table. "Let's get started. The guy from 'Rock Anthem' will be here in a couple of hours."

"Yeah," Skins agreed. "We need to have all the pictures nailed down by the end of the week, so we need to crack on."

Tom and Jake looked at each other and started to laugh.

"God they're such grown-ups aren't they?" Jake said.

"I know, they never let us have any fun. Why don't you ever let us have any fun?" Tom whined like a child.

"We do," Luke protested. "We always let you have fun, don't we Skins?"

Skins looked affronted at their claim. "Luke and I are full of fun. You just forget because you two are idiots *all* the time."

"Okay," Tom said. "Tell me one time when you two have had fun without us."

Skins and Luke looked at each other, both staring wide eyed, communicating silently.

"I'm not telling them that," Luke insisted.

"But we have nothing else," Skins hissed.

"Yeah, but we swore we wouldn't mention it again."

"Oh, now you have to tell us," Jake chimed in. "You know if you don't we'll just hound you and grind you down until you do tell us."

Luke eyed Skins warily. "It's up to you."

Skins hesitated and then said. "Okay, but if Stacey or Martha ever find out, you two are dead to us. I mean it."

Tom nodded vigorously, while Jake crossed himself.

"Okay," Skins said, "It happened about three years ago."

CHAPTER 11

♥

3 YEARS EARLIER

Dirty Riches had launched a foundation that provided holidays and summer camps for children from within the social care system, and everyone wanted to talk to them about it. This meant that Jake and Tom had gone to Glasgow to do a radio interview, while Skins and Luke were doing a TV guest slot on a mid-morning show in London. That was why the lead singer and drummer were stumbling down a hotel corridor, bouncing from wall to wall like a pinball. They'd had dinner, accompanied by two bottles of wine, followed by a couple of brandies each and were both were fairly well oiled.

"Shit, that wine was lethal," Luke hiccupped.

"Yep." Skins pulled to a stop, did a huge belch and thumped his chest with a closed fist. "Sorry, the garlic prawns just popped up to say hi."

"Fucking hell, Skins. I can smell it." Luke pushed at Skins' shoulder and groaned.

"Said I was sorry."

They continued down the corridor, making a turn towards the door for their suite, when Luke collided with a woman. She was almost as tall as him, was wearing a tight, bottle-green dress and had a mass of auburn curls.

"Oof sorry," Luke said, holding his hands up.

"No problem," the woman replied, flashing him a bright-white veneer smile. "We were wondering where you were. We knocked a couple of times, didn't we Greg?"

She took a step to the side to reveal a man dressed in a charcoal grey suit, with a black open-necked shirt.

"Hey," the man, Greg, said, giving an equally perfect smile and waving a hand.

Luke looked him up and down, and noticing the camera bag over his shoulder, guessed they were here to do an interview about the foundation. He quickly turned to Skins and grimaced.

"I must have forgotten," he hissed. "Did Neil say anything to you?"

"Nope." Skins took a deep breath and braced himself against the wall.

Luke shook his head and turned back to the couple who were watching them intently.

"Sorry about that, we'd forgotten you were coming." He reached into the back pocket of his jeans for the key card, cursing Neil for organising an interview at ten at night, and for himself for not replacing Lily, his last PA who'd left to travel Australia with her boyfriend a month ago-something that Luke thought was stupid, as she could travel the whole bloody world with the band, for free.

"No problem," the woman purred, placing a flat palm on Luke's back.

Luke stiffened and looked back over his shoulder at her. She was attractive admittedly, but he really didn't want her touching him. That was how things got misconstrued and ended up in newspapers, and that was not something he wanted to deal with. Shrugging away her touch, Luke opened the door and let them inside the suite of a lounge, kitchen and two en-suite bedrooms. As he walked into the lounge the side lights came on automatically, casting a soft glow around the room.

"Please take a seat...sorry I didn't catch your name or where you're from."

The woman moved over to one of the dove grey

leather couches and lowered herself down demurely. "Penny and we're from Masquerade. We spoke to your assistant, Lucy."

Luke nodded in understanding, but not understanding at all. What sort of magazine was called Masquerade, and why had Lily not added this to his diary before she'd left?

"When did you speak to her?" he asked, shrugging of his jacket.

"Yesterday."

Luke frowned, well it definitely wasn't Lily as she was currently on a sheep ranch in the Australian outback. Maybe his mamma had taken the call-perhaps they misheard Lucy instead of Lucia.

"Okay, well you're here now." Turning to Skins, Luke wobbled slightly. Shit, he really needed to get some coffee inside him, and by the look of him Skins needed it even more so. His friend was gripping onto the back of the other couch and had a glazed look on his face. They really were out of practice at drinking alcohol. They only drank bottled beer these days, never the hard stuff, in fact he and Skins had been on a complete alcohol ban for the last two months. It had started out as an argument with Jake about who drank the most, and quickly turned into a bet that neither of them could last two months without an alcoholic drink. The previous day had been the two-month marker, which was why they'd gone mad over dinner.

"I'll make us all some coffee. Sit down, before you fall down," he whispered to Skins as he passed.

A few minutes later, Luke came back with a pot of fresh coffee, cups and milk. He placed the tray carefully on the low coffee table, making sure to concentrate on keeping himself balanced as he bent over. As he did, he was sure he felt something move up the back of his leg, but when he looked around Penny was busy talking to Skins, while Greg listened. To be fair, she was talking *at* Skins as he was trying hard not to let his head loll to the side and was fighting to keep his eyes open.

As Luke sat down on the sofa, Penny moved a little closer to him, resting a hand on his thigh.

"Shall we get down to business?" she asked, glancing over at Greg who had his arm along the back of the couch behind Skins.

Crossing his leg over to lose Penny's hand, Luke cleared his throat. "Are you going to record it?" he asked, noticing that Penny hadn't taken any notepad out of her bag.

Penny tilted her head to one side and licked her bottom lip. "Would you like us to?"

"I have the equipment," Greg added, nodding towards his bag that was now on the floor. "You'd have no need to worry, it would be strictly confidential."

"Until it goes public," Luke replied, furrowing his brow.

"Honestly, don't worry about it. You'd have the only copy." Greg shifted in his seat, moving closer to Skins.

"What the-." Skins eyes shot open as though he'd been electrocuted and turned to Greg. "Did you just tickle my ear?" He flapped a hand at the side of his head, as though swatting a fly and then let out another belch, much louder than the last one.

Luke groaned. This was going to be an awful interview. He wouldn't blame them if they portrayed him and Skins as a pair of drunks, who could barely string two words together. They needed to collect themselves, otherwise this would be really bad publicity for the foundation. Leaning forward, Luke poured some coffee and then passed one to Skins.

"Drink this."

With a shaky hand, Skins took the cup and raised it to his lips, took a gulp and blew out a breath.

"Don't you have anything stronger?" Greg asked, as he took a cup from Luke but placed it directly back down onto the table.

"Well there's the mini bar. What would you like?"

Penny rubbed her foot against Luke's calf. "Maybe later. We have plenty of things to help you loosen up."

"Oh, we'll be fine," Luke replied, not liking the gold, stiletto shoe touching him, or the thought of a game of quick fire twenty questions-something a few journalists had done with them at the beginning of their career to try and relax them into their interview. "We've done this many, many times."

"Ah, okay. Lucy gave us the impression you were fairly new to this," Penny said.

Luke was a little surprised that Lucia would say that. Also, how did Penny not realise how seasoned they were at giving interviews. They'd been one of the world's biggest rock bands for almost twenty years.

"How do you want to do this?" Penny asked, moving to the edge of her seat. "Together or separately? If it's separately we'd prefer to have the doors open and unlocked. We're not casting aspersions, but we've had some real hairy moments where one of us had needed help-you know the sort of guy we're talking about, likes to get rough. So, we need to be able to get to each other should we require assistance."

"What the fuck," Luke muttered. "What type of people do you deal with?"

Penny giggled and rubbed his back. "All sorts, we're highly experienced."

Then, without any warning, Luke felt his shirt being pulled up, and a hand going down the back of his jeans, as Penny leaned into him while pulling at a tie at the waist of her dress with her other hand.

"What?"

As Luke tried to stand up, Penny's hand tightened on the waistband of his boxer briefs and she pulled him back down onto the couch.

"Not so fast," she cooed. "Let's start out here, we can move to the bedroom in a few."

"No!" he cried. "This isn't-"

Before he had time to finish, Skins let out a roar and pushed up from the coach.

"What the fuck do you think you're doing?" he bellowed, staggering backwards and tripping over the coffee table, he swayed precariously before landing in a heap amidst the cups and coffee pot.

"You sure you've done this before?" Greg asked, standing up and throwing his jacket behind him. "You're both a little jittery."

Skins eyes widened as Greg started to unbutton his shirt. "What are you doing?"

"Come on," Penny said, running her hands through Luke's hair. "Let's get you relaxed."

"My fucking hair." Luke pushed her hand away and managed to stand up.

"Greg," she said, turning to the now bare-chested man. "Get the poppers, someone is a little tense." She giggled and with a quick tug, her dress opened to reveal a black, lace bra with the nipples cut out and the tiniest black lace triangle for a pair of knickers.

"What? No!" Luke bellowed. "What the hell?"

"Shit, get him off me."

Luke turned to see Greg was now dressed only in a red sequined G-string and was straddling Skins, rubbing his hands up and down the drummer's broad chest.

"Get off him." Luke leaned over to push Greg off, lost his balance and fell face down over the coffee table. His head was in line with Greg's bare arse that was sticking up in the air as he continued his massage of Skins.

"Leave me the fuck alone," Skins shouted, pushing at Greg. "This is assault you mother-fucking dickhead. What the fuck do you think you're doing?"

Greg must have seen the anger in Skins' eyes, because he paused, looked at him and then turned to Luke who was trying to push himself up from the table.

"You did use the name, Mr Rigley to book us, right?" he asked.

"What the fuck are you talking about?" Luke replied, his arms stretched out as he held himself up. "And who the fuck are you?"

Just as Greg opened his mouth to answer, a loud yelp was heard and, a now totally naked Penny, landed on Luke's back and started to buck against his back, as she swung her bra around in the air.

"Come on sexy, relax. Let Penny show you a good time," she called.

"Oh shit," Greg groaned. "God I'm so sorry. We were told to go to the penthouse suite of the Monarch Crown Hotel."

Luke's body jerked as Penny continued to ride him. "Well for one this isn't the penthouse suite and for two it's the fucking Monarch Royal Hotel. The Crown is the other side of Hyde Park you dick. Now get her the fuck off me."

"Penny! Stop!" Greg's voice was loud and deep, and instantly Penny stopped her gyrating.

"What?" she asked, while pinching her nipples.

"We're in the wrong place. This is the wrong hotel."

Penny gasped and looked at Luke, who was peering at her over his shoulder. "You didn't give the alias of Mr Rigley?"

"No, I've already said. Now get off me."

She didn't move except to slap a hand over her face. "Oh my God. I'm so sorry."

"Yes, we're really sorry," Greg added, his hand over his heart.

"That's fucking great man," Skins growled. "But do you think you could get the fuck off my junk, it's shrivelled to fucking nothing as it is, but the longer I have to look at your red sparkly crotch, the more likelihood I'll be fucking impotent for life."

Greg looked down at said red, sparkly crotch and inhaled. "Oh God, I'm so sorry." He jumped up and started to grab for his clothes. "Penny get dressed. Now!"

Penny followed suit and pushed off Luke, reaching behind for her clothes and starting to pull them back on. Within a couple of minutes they were out of the door, babbling their apologies and begging not to be sued.

"What the hell made you think they were here to interview us?" Skins asked, now totally sober.

"I just assumed. He looked like he'd got a camera, and we've done that many interviews over the last few weeks, I thought it was another one." Luke rubbed a hand over his face as he flopped down onto the couch.

"Oh, he had a camera alright. A fucking video camera to record us doing the nasty with them. Ugh," Skins grimaced. "I feel defiled."

"I know, I need to scrub my body with bleach. And I'm burning this fucking t-shirt where she's rubbed her pussy against it. It was probably rancid."

"I won't sleep tonight. Every time I close my eyes, I'll see a fucking red, glittery ball sack in front of me."

They sat in silence for a few minutes, both trying to calm down from their ordeal, when there was a knock at the door.

"If that's them come back for more, I'll fucking punch him in the bollocks," Skins said as he pushed up from the couch and strode to the door.

He swung it open and almost fell over in shock.

"Surprise!" was the chorus from Stacey and Martha.

"W-what are you doing here?" he asked, pulling Stacey into a one-armed hug, while his other hand gripped the door.

"We thought it was an ideal opportunity to get

some adult time. Abbie and Amber have gone to Glasgow too."

Luke appeared behind Skins and clutched at his hair. If they'd arrived ten minutes earlier no doubt he and Skins would be heading for a divorce.

"Baby," he managed to utter.

Martha pushed passed Stacey and Skins and skipped up to him, jumping up and wrapping her legs around his waist.

"I missed you. I know I only saw you this morning, but I really, really missed you. I think it was the excitement at knowing that we'd have a night all to ourselves-no kids sneaking into our bed at four in the morning."

Luke let out a breath and hugged her tight. "Fuck, it's so good to see you."

He looked at Skins over the top of Martha's head, and as Stacey was also enveloped in a hug, she didn't see the look of relief pass between them.

Luke carried Martha into the suite and as they got inside, he hugged her tighter and kissed her hard and deep.

"Wow," she sighed, eventually pulling away. "That was a really, really good welcome."

"I'm so happy you're here, that's all."

"Hey," Skins said from behind them. "Did you know your auntie Thelma was at your house, helping your mum with all the kids?"

"What all of them?" Luke asked astonished.

Martha nodded. "Yes, but Gabriella has gone too, and she said we don't have to go back until the day after tomorrow."

"My sister is officially nuts," Luke said with a laugh. "All the kids are bad enough, but Mamma and Thelma as well. Christ she'll be ready to kill them by the time we get back." Thinking about it, Luke dropped his head back and let out a loud laugh. As he did so his heart stopped and dropped with a thud to his stomach. Hanging from the lampshade was a black, lace bra that distinctly looked like the nipples were cut out.

He could think of nothing but the words 'Fuck my life.'

CHAPTER 12

PRESENT DAY

As Luke finished regaling his tale, Jake was doubled over laughing. Tom however looked bemused.

"You pair of idiots," Jake said when he eventually stopped laughing. "Why didn't you ask to see their press cards before you let them in?"

Luke shrugged. "Like I said, we'd done so many fucking interviews I just thought it was another one that Neil had arranged."

"Plus, we were so pissed, we weren't really on the ball." Skins reached over to the bag of pastries on the table and took out another croissant. "These are great, where did you get them from?"

Luke shrugged. "Don't know, just sent out for them." He looked at Tom, who was silently watching them. "What's wrong with you, not got anything to say?"

"She ran her fingers through your hair. Fuck, how did she manage to escape with you not breaking them?"

Luke stared open mouthed at Tom.

"That story was fucking hilarious sugar tits and the main thing you took from it was that some chick ran her fingers through Luke's hair."

"Yeah. *And* she survived to tell the tale," Tom replied.

"She better not have fucking done," Luke groaned. "Tell the tale, I mean."

"Neil made them sign a legal document, they won't have dared spill." Skins took a large bite of his pastry, finishing it off with a lick of his fingers. "So fucking good," he said around a mouthful of food.

"You told Neil, but not us?" Jake asked, slightly affronted.

"Err yeah. You've got a bigger mouth than the Hudson river," Luke replied. "Tom what the fuck is wrong with you."

Tom was shaking his head and muttering to himself.

"I just can't believe you let her touch your hair.

You almost punched me in the throat when I did it that one time."

"No, that was because you annoy the fuck out of me-a lot. The hair touching was an excuse."

"So, I can touch it now then?" Tom asked, taking a step towards Luke.

"No!" Luke gasped. "No, you can't." He lifted a hand and smoothed it slowly over his hair, looked at Tom and then visibly shuddered.

"Well whatever, that story is funny as fuck," Jake sighed. "But you still weren't having fun, were you. It was more of a horror story."

"It's funny now, looking back on it. The look on Luke's face when he saw the bra hanging from the lampshade was the funniest thing ever."

"You didn't think so at the time." Luke poked at Skins' chest. "If I remember you nearly shit your pants and couldn't get Stacey into your bedroom quick enough."

"No, I was relaxed about the whole thing. You were the one stressing out, I just wanted to be inside my wife."

"Whatever," Luke said waving a dismissive hand at his friend.

"How did you get it down?" Tom asked, taking one of the take-out coffees from the tray.

"I woke *him* up in the middle of the night," Luke replied, pointing at Skins. "Got on his shoulders and got it down."

"What did you do with it-keep it in your undies drawer for safe keeping?"

"Fuck off Jake. No, we put it in the elevator and sent it down to reception."

They all started to laugh, imagining the poor night porter's face at the sight of a black, lace, bra arriving in reception.

"Ah well, maybe you do have some fun without us," Jake sighed. "Not much though."

"Yeah, you're probably right." Luke moved over to the photographs and looked through them, separating some out. "Shit, where the fuck have the years gone?"

"I know. It's gone by so fast. I remember that first day seeing you at college. You thought you were so cool."

Luke shook his head. "Jake I'm still fucking cool now, my sons are cool and my dad was cool-it's in our blood."

"You're so right," Jake mocked.

He then sighed and thought back to that day. He'd known Tom from school, although they'd never really spoken to each other that much. Luke and Skins though were already friends, living close to each other, and when they found themselves in the same music lesson they all gravitated together-Dirty Riches were most definitely meant to happen. Thank God they were, because without them Jake wasn't sure he'd have stayed out of trouble.

"You guys saved me, you know that right?" he said, emotion building in his gut.

"No, we didn't," Skins said, rubbing Jakes head. "You'd have been famous no matter whether you'd been in a band or not. Someone with an ego the size of yours couldn't be anything else."

"Nah, I'd have ended up in bother-maybe even prison."

"I don't remember you being like that at school," Tom said. "I know we didn't really mix in the same circles, but you didn't strike me as being a troublemaker."

"I'd have rebelled eventually. My dad was suck a prick, it was bound to come out in me somehow. Looking after Mum was so stressful and so damn tiring, I'd have probably cracked. Being in the band meant I could get away without feeling guilty. I could tell myself I was doing it for her, to help her have a better life, but really it was for myself."

"You had nothing to be guilty about buddy," Luke said. "You'd looked after her for years. You don't blame yourself for her-"

Jake shook his head. "God, no. I blame her. Same thing I said to Freckles a while back. I blame my mum, for taking the pills and for not loving me enough to stay. She loved that fucker of my father more, even though he wasn't even there and hadn't been for years. She couldn't live without him, but she could me, her son. The one who loved and cared for her."

Jake's mother suffered from deep depression for years, mainly through his dad abandoning them. Her highs and happy times were sporadic, and when she was low and in a deep, dark pit of hopelessness it took Jake all his time to simply get her to dress or eat. When the band started she was doing better, but when they signed their record deal Jake knew she was slipping back.

"I ignored it you know."

"What?" Tom asked.

"When we signed the deal. I could see the signs that she was getting bad again, but like the selfish prick I was I ignored it and hoped she'd pull through. And she did, or so I thought."

"What do you mean buddy?" Luke asked, his eyes full of concern.

"She was hiding it from me. Hiding the fact that the darkness was back. Or maybe yet again I'd chosen to ignore it." He let out a long sigh. "Who knows, I just know that the day I got word she'd killed herself I thought my heart had been ripped from my chest."

"Shit, I remember it like it was yesterday." Tom placed a comforting hand on Jake's shoulder. "As soon as Neil walked into the dressing room and said he wanted to speak to you, you went deathly white."

"Yeah, I just knew."

Jake's eyes filled with tears as he thought of about

it, and the ache in his chest was as bad as it had been that day.

CHAPTER 13

♥

16 YEARS EARLIER

The band had just finished a concert in front of a packed arena, and as they did every night, had left the stage to screams for more – even though they'd already done two encores. All of them were hot and sweaty and were swigging back bottles of beer in the dressing room.

"Did you see that girl with the huge tits?" Tom asked, wiping a towel up his face and across his head. "When she whipped her top off my dick woke up."

"How can you get a hard on at a pair of tits in the

crowd." Skins shook his head and gulped back the rest of his beer.

"Yeah, sugar tits. Was the blowie you got, just before we went on, not enough for you?"

"I did not get a blowie," Tom protested. "She'd dropped her pen that I was signing her tits with."

"More tits! Fucking hell, Tom. You're tit obsessed." Luke laughed as Tom flipped him the bird.

"He's a titaholic," Skins added.

"He is a tit," Jake quipped, ducking to avoid a smack across the back of the head from Tom.

After their laughter died down, they continued drinking in silence, nodding at Neil as he came into the room.

"Hey guys, good show," he said quietly, scratching at the back of his neck. "Jake, you got a minute?"

When Jake saw Neil's face, dread registered inside of him. He dropped his bottle of beer onto the table, letting it land with a loud thud. His heart started to beat ten times the normal speed and he could hear the blood pumping in his ears.

"Mum," he whispered.

Neil nodded his head. "I'm so sorry Jake. A neighbour found her, she'd arranged to go to the supermarket with her and when Eliza didn't show she went round to the house. She had a key apparently."

"H-how?" Jake asked, clearing his throat and dropping down onto a chair. He dragged the beanie hat from his head and gripped it tightly, twisting it in his hands.

"Jake, really you don't-."

"No Neil," Jake snapped. "I need to know."

"It was tablets and vodka. The police said she'd been dead for about twelve hours."

"Fuck." Jake dropped his head back and looked up at the ceiling. He stared at the stains, probably made by beer and all manner of other things being thrown around by bands and pop stars over the years. "She didn't want to be found then, otherwise she'd have taken it just before Denise arrived. I take it that it was Denise?" he asked, looking at Neil.

"I don't know Jake. The police just said it was a neighbour."

"Yeah." Jake nodded, looking into the distance. "It would be Denise. They've been friends for a while. Since I bought the place for mum."

"Jake, buddy. What do you want to do?" Luke asked, placing a comforting hand on Jake's back. "What can we do for you?"

Jake looked up at him, his eyes full of tears. "I don't know, Luke. I-" The damn broke and deep, wracking sobs broke from deep within Jake's chest. He rocked in his chair, trying to gulp in air as tears and snot mixed together and ran down his face. Luke pulled Jake up and engulfed him in a tight embrace. Holding his brother against him, taking in his sorrow and trying to give him strength.

Jake felt the comfort of Luke's arms, but his chest ached with the pain. His mum was gone and he'd never see her pretty face, with the tired blue eyes again. The thought of the despair she must have been in, dragged a shuddering breath from his lungs and he let out a howl of pain. She'd been alone in her darkness-alone, scared and with all hope lost. His father's desertion of them years ago, was what had sent her spiralling down. He had done this.

"Why Luke?" he sobbed. "Why let that fucker win?"

At the sound of his friend's anguish, Skins quickly moved over to them and wrapped his arms around his two friends, closely followed by Tom. Blowing out a breath, Tom let Skins pull him into their tight group. Brothers and best friends all mourning with one of their own.

Neil pinched the bridge of his nose as he considered the consequences of what had happened. Jake was strong, but this was not something anyone would find it easy to deal with. Particularly as for most of his life Jake had been Eliza's carer. He'd been the strong one, desperately trying to get her through each day, but this would hit him hard. While he felt guilty thinking about it, he had to consider the rest of the tour too. They had three dates left on this current leg and then two months off. He didn't want to have to ask the boys what they wanted to do, but he *had* to and it needed to be tonight in case they decided to cancel.

After giving them a few more minutes, Neil cleared his throat.

"I hate to do this guys, but I need to know what you want to do about the remaining three dates."

Luke extracted himself from the huddle and rounded on Neil. "Really? You're asking that now?"

"I know it's bad timing, Luke, but I have to let the venue know tonight, if you're going to cancel."

"Bad timing doesn't really cut it, Neil. And, of course we're cancelling. In respect to Eliza."

The band had got to know each other's families well over the years, and Eliza Hughes had always been a welcome backstage visitor, or guest at any parties they'd thrown for their friends and families. She was a petite, blonde with a fractured soul and a frail demeanour and the boys loved and protected her – she was Jake's mum, so there was no question of it.

"No," Jake said, rubbing his arm under his nose. "She wouldn't have wanted us to let all the fans down. We go ahead as planned. I just need to go home tomorrow, Neil. Can you arrange that?"

Neil nodded. "Yes, no problem son."

Jake gave him a watery smile. He liked that Neil called them all son. They all had fathers of their own, although his own was a fucking dead loss, but Neil calling them son meant he cared about them. He was so much more than a manager in many ways and Margo, his wife, adored them all –despite the trouble they more often than not caused her husband.

No, Jake knew that this was a hard thing for Neil to ask. He would be feeling Jake's pain as much as Luke, Tom and Skins were.

"Are you sure?" Tom asked, placing a flat palm on Jakes head, almost cradling it. "We're happy to cancel."

"Maybe we can get a stand in for you?" Skins suggested.

Jake let out a huff of breath. "Like who? No one can play that riff in Poisonous Love like I can, and as for Shattered Lives, well even Tom can't play the guitar solo as well as me, and he wrote the fucking thing. Nope, not happening."

Skins sighed and nodded. "Okay buddy. Neil, we do everything necessary for Jake to get home. Can you organise a flight for him tonight? We'll go back on the tour bus and meet him at the venue tomorrow night."

They were currently in Glasgow and the last three nights would be in Manchester- the city they considered as their home. Neil gave a short nod – he would hire a private plane to get Jake home if he had to.

"Tom, you go with him." Neil said, knowing that Jake would need some support. Tom, despite his stupidity at times was probably the strongest of them all. The one least likely to lose it. The one who would be a greater strength to Jake.

Tom agreed. "Yep, wouldn't want to be anywhere else." He slapped Jake's back. "Come on buddy let's get our stuff off the bus."

Jake nodded and wiped at his eyes. He looked at the four men in the room with him, and breathed a sigh of thankfulness. He loved them all and wouldn't want any other men around him at such an awful time. They would always stand by him-something that his mum simply didn't have the strength to do. They were his brothers, his bandmates – they were now the only family he had.

CHAPTER 14

♥

PRESENT DAY

Three was a loud knock on the door, stirring everyone from their reverie. They each looked to the door as it opened and Olivia popped her head around.

"Your visitor is here."

Luke smiled and nodded. "Cheers, Liv. Send him in, oh could you make us some fresh coffee please."

Olivia nodded, taking the empty take-out cups handed to her by Luke, she quietly closed the door behind her. A couple of minutes later, the door opened again and she ushered in a tall man wearing black cargo pants, a long-sleeved Henley, and black Oakley sunglasses perched on top of his head. He was carrying a backpack over one shoulder and a camera case over the other.

"Hey, guys. I'm Mike Davenport from Rock Anthem." He held his hand out to Jake, who was the first one in line.

"Hey Mike," Jake replied. "Great to meet you, but can I see your press pass please?"

Mike's brow furrowed. "Er, yeah no problem."

"Sorry Mike, it's just that we've had people pretend to be press before, and…let's just say it wasn't pleasant."

"Jake," Luke growled. "Ignore him Mike, I saw your credentials when the magazine emailed them over yesterday."

"What?" Jake asked, grinning from ear to ear. "He might be a hooker for all we know."

Mike gave a short, uncomfortable laugh. "I'm not, I can assure you."

"Yes, we know." Luke gave him a tight smile, at the same time as poking Jake in the back. "He thinks he's funny."

"I *am* funny," Jake muttered under his breath, loud enough for them all to hear. "I'm funny aren't I Tom?"

Tom let out a sigh, not wanting to be brought into one of Jake's comedic routines, but relieved that he hadn't been called Sugar Tits, and nodded.

"Hilarious."

"See, Tom thinks I'm hilarious."

"Great to meet you, Mike." Throwing Jake a look of disdain, Skins stepped forward and shook Mike's hand.

Luke and Tom followed suit and then everyone sat down on the couches-Mike on one in between Luke and Skins. Luke looked across at Jake and gave him a warning glare, telling him silently to behave. Jake nudged Tom.

"Do you see it Thomas, how the older brothers always sit together. Always leaving us to our own devices." Jake's tone was light and mocking, but Mike's head shot up from searching through his backpack.

"Is that how you see yourselves?" he asked. "Two different factions of the one band?"

"No!" They all chorused.

"No, definitely not," Luke added. "Like I said, Jake thinks he's funny."

Mike looked at them in turn, before nodding and going back to searching through his bag. Luke in the meantime, pointed an accusing finger at Jake and narrowed his eyes at him. After a few minutes, Mike appeared to have everything that he needed.

"Okay," he said, placing a plastic file on the coffee table. "Today is really to determine the angle of the interview and to decide how in depth and raw you're willing to go. I don't believe in showing my questions beforehand," he said opening up a notepad. "It loses all the spontaneity of the interview, but I also don't want the interview to become uncomfortable because I've asked you something that you're not happy answering. There's nothing worse than an interview room that's highly charged with displeasure, lack of trust and anger. I won't write a decent interview and none of us will be happy, including my editor, or my readers."

"So, basically," Skins replied. "You want to see how much dirt we're willing to give you."

Mike nodded. "Yep, that's it. I'd also like to find out how you want to do it, together or individually or a mixture of both. Ultimately, you guys are rock royalty. You deserve an exceptional piece in the magazine, so I want to make sure we get that."

They all nodded, and each in turn visibly relaxed. One by one, sitting back in the couch, unfolding their arms and uncrossing their legs.

"What were your thoughts then?" Luke asked. "You know, on how you wanted the interview to go?"

Mike leaned forward, opened the file and took out some papers, handing one to each of the men. "These are some pivotal points in your career - areas that I'd like to cover. For each of those points there'll be a series of questions. Either directly about the incident, or around the aftermath."

"Sounds serious," Tom replied, looking down at

the sheet of paper.

"They're not all serious or hard subjects, I promise. You'll see that Skins' addiction and subsequent collapse, is one of those points."

"We knew it would be," Skins said. "And while I know it's an important part of our history, I have kids and don't really want them to learn all about how their dad would have cut off his arm to get a fix, at the same time as disrespecting their mother by being a total coke-headed prick."

Luke reached behind Mike to place a hand on Skins' shoulder. "You don't have to answer anything you don't want to buddy."

"Mr Mahoney is right, Mr Ballard," Mike replied. "But you're right too, it's an important part of your history."

"We can talk about it, but I'll refuse anything that I'm not comfortable with, and will discuss with the guys what I'm willing for them to say. And please, Mike, it's Luke, Skins, Tom and Jake."

Mike nodded. "Okay. Thank you. So, having a quick look at the sheet are there any subjects on there that any of you are not willing to talk about?"

Silently they each read the paper that Mike had given to them. Tom looked up and scratched his head.

"I'm not so sure I want the kiss and tell story by Morgan Laketon mentioned."

"Right, and why is that?" Mike asked. "I'm not

trying to be difficult, I'd like to know your reason so we can discuss how it could be turned into a positive."

"Hah, believe me," Tom scoffed. "There was nothing positive about that skank."

"I agree with Tom," Jake said. "She's not important in our story. She simply wanted notoriety and money and had no impact on our career, other than the fifteen minutes of fame that she got from it. I'm not happy with her being discussed here in this room, never mind being included in the interview."

"It *was* a huge story at the time. She not only sold her story and some pictures, but also intimated it was against her will."

Tom pushed up from the couch and screwed up the sheet of paper, angrily throwing it in Mike's direction.

"Yeah and if that's the angle you're fucking taking then I won't take any part in the interview. There was no fucking substance to that and that couple who were in the next room proved that."

Tom moved over to the table where the photographs were laid out, and only just stopped himself from upturning the lot. His heart was beating wildly and threatening to break free from his chest, he was so angry. Abbie knew all about that night, and what Morgan-fucking-Laketon had done, but he did not want to be dragged back to the grimy surface of that whore's life. Tainting the goodness that he had going on. The beauty that his wife and daughter gave to him.

"I'm sorry, Tom," Mike said breaking into his thoughts. "I totally understand your feelings, and we can cut it. I wanted to know how that affected you as a band. Did it impact on you and your life - did you change because of it?"

Tom swung around and glared at Mike. "Of course we fucking changed. Me particularly, I was the one she tried to say had forced her. Would you stay the same if some woman claimed you'd back-handed her and threatened her with more violence if she didn't take part in a threesome?"

"Okay, it's cut." Mike nodded and scribbled across his copy of the list.

"Come on, Tom," Luke said in a cajoling tone. "Sit back down and let's go through the rest of the list."

"I am sorry, Tom. But you have to understand, I'm a journalist, it's my job to ask difficult questions."

Tom scrubbed a hand down his face as he sat back down. "I know that," he sighed. "It was just an awful situation and I really don't want to relive it or have my wife have to hear any more about it than she already has. I'm not trying to re-write history, but I don't think she's relevant."

"I have to agree," Skins added. "My addiction caused the band to have to take time out for a while, Morgan Layton didn't change us as a band. Yeah, she made life difficult and could have ruined Tom, but she didn't because she was a money-grabbing, rancid bitch who doesn't deserve any more air time."

"Okay, gents. Point taken. So, what about the rest of the list?"

Olivia bought coffee in, and for the next couple of hours they discussed the list, added some other points and removed a couple of others that might upset their wives - namely one-night stands and groupies - and agreed on the format. They'd all be interviewed together and then individually on their thoughts on their band-mates.

Having finalised his format Mike shook each of their hands and left.

"You think he'll stick to what we've agreed on?" Tom asked.

"Yeah," Luke replied, pouring himself more coffee from the fresh pot that Olivia had brought in. "One, we have final say before publication. Two, if he does print something we've not agreed to, Neil will see he gets blacklisted so that the only job he'll get, will be writing ads for Auto Trader. Don't worry about it. Morgan Laketon will not be mentioned."

"Good," Tom muttered as he dropped his head back on the couch and closed his eyes.

"Of course," Jake said, as he nudged an elbow against Tom. "We all know it's because my performance that night was far superior to yours."

Tom's eyes remained closed, his head still resting on the couch, but his hand shot up and slapped Jake around the back of the head.

"Shut the fuck up, dickweed."

They all laughed, but Tom felt unease deep in his gut as he thought about that night, and the woman who had sold her story to the press about it. That hadn't bothered him, after all he was a rock star in his prime – plenty of other rock stars had had threesomes with a band member and had their story sold. No, the dread that rushed through his veins was the story that Tom had forced her, with a slap, to take part. He hadn't at all, but the damn bitch had intimated that in her 'tell all' story to a Sunday newspaper. Thankfully, the next day the couple in the next room to him and Jake had come forward and said they'd heard her literally begging the boys to 'do her' at the same time. They'd even admitted to going into the corridor and listening at the wall and laughing about her administrations of 'need to be done by two rock stars'. It still hadn't stopped the paper who'd run her story, trying to say the couple had been paid off, but Neil had soon sorted that one out. The young couple had found her moaning so hilarious, they'd taped it on one of their mobile phones and it was quite clear that in no way whatsoever, Ms Laketon was forced. Neil had then slapped the paper with a law suit of slander – or libel, Tom could never remember which. It still filled him with dread at the thought. If the couple hadn't come forward things might have been very different.

"As a matter of interest," Skins said, kicking at

Tom's outstretched leg. "How many threesomes have you two had together?"

"Just that one," Jake replied. "To be honest, watching Tom shoot his load over someone's back wasn't exactly my idea of sexual nirvana."

Tom opened his eyes and lifted his head. "Oh, and me watching you get blown off by lips thicker than a tractor inner tube was fun for me? No, I don't think so."

"What about you two?" Jake nodded at Skins and Luke. "You ever dabbled?"

They both shook their heads.

"Nah, Luke would be intimidated by the length and girth of my dick for starters."

"Hah," Luke snorted derisively. "As if. I've never had any complaints. I have had threesomes but never with another man. Not my sort of thing."

"Me neither. Not surprised you two did though - you were fucking joined at the hip most of the time."

"I know," Jake sighed. "He's like a fucking limpet. I can't get rid of him."

"Whatever."

"He only stuck with me so I could pull the girls for him. He'd still be a virgin now if it wasn't for my tutelage."

"If that's what you want to believe, Jake, then you do that." Tom grinned as a memory came into his mind. "I do believe it was the beautiful Mrs Brady who started me on the path to righteousness."

"Ah the mythical Mrs Brady."

"Oh, she exists, Luke. I promise you."

They all started to laugh. Tom even had a Gibson Les Paul guitar named after the older woman who had taken his virginity.

"Go on then," Jake said faking a yawn. "Tells us again how she sorted you out."

"I've told you before. I'm not telling you again just so you can get a hard on and rub one out in the office bathroom."

"You've never told us the full story," Skins replied. "Only that you lost your virginity to her, which kinda makes me think that without the detail there is none."

"Yeah, Skins is right," Luke added. "We've never actually had the gory detail."

Tom sighed and shook his head. "Okay, if you really want to know."

CHAPTER 15

♥

24 YEARS EARLIER

"Okay, I'll be there," Tom hissed down the phone line. "I've got to go and cut a customer's lawn, but I swear I'll be there on time."

"Make sure you are," Luke replied. "We've got the gig at college in two weeks and we've hardly rehearsed at all."

"Alright, alright. If you stop moaning and let me go I'd be able to get it done a lot quicker and make sure I'm on time."

"Right, I'm going. Don't be late."

The line went dead and Tom replaced the receiver with a muttered curse.

"Who was that Thomas?" His mother asked, coming into the hall wiping her hands on a tea towel.

"Just Luke reminding me we've got band rehearsal later."

Tom flicked his shaggy fringe from out of his eyes and gave her a tight smile. If he knew his mum, she was going to start complaining about the time he spent with the band when he should be studying.

"Don't you have Mrs Brady's lawn to do?"

Okay, so she wasn't going with the studying, but it was still her way of telling him not to waste his time.

"Yeah, I'm goin' now."

"It's yes, and going, with a G, Thomas. I do wish you'd speak properly."

Tom's lips twitched at the corners into a small smile. "Sorry. I'm going now," he said, emphasising the G.

Brenda, his mother, sighed and then turned back down the hall to the kitchen. Evidently, she couldn't be bothered to argue today. Taking his opportunity, Tom took his backpack from the coat hook on the wall, picked up his guitar case, opened the front door and ran down the path. His backpack had a change of clothes, a can of coke and a cheese and onion pasty in it. Everything he needed to avoid having to go home after doing Mrs Brady's lawn.

As he ran through the estate to Mrs Brady's house,

a few streets away, he started to get hard thinking about her. At twenty-seven-years of age, she was only ten years older than him-well nine years and eleven months as he would be eighteen soon. The age gap didn't matter to Tom, as far as he was concerned she was magnificent. With her long legs, undulating curves and long black hair, she was like a Disney princess on steroids. In other words, she was sexy as fuck and her body was the image in his head every time he rubbed one out - which was getting to be twice a day recently.

Within five minutes, Tom had reached the corner of her road, where he pulled to a stop. Glancing over at her house, he lifted his arms and gave his armpits a quick sniff. Yep, they were fine, but for good measure he reached inside his bag, pulled out his aerosol deodorant and gave himself another quick spray. Coughing, as he'd been a little too liberal, he shoved it back into his bag, smoothed back his shaggy hair and sedately walked over to number 33 Primrose Close - the place where all his dreams were made.

Straightening his t-shirt, Tom knocked on the door and waited. He knew the drill. He'd see the outline of Mrs Brady's curves through the frosted glass of the front door. Halfway down the hall, she'd realise it was Tom and for the last couple of feet there'd be an extra sway to her hips. Then, when she opened the front door, she'd smile, lick her lips and then push her big tits out until her nipples were straining at the fabric of whatever top she was wearing - usually something with a low neck that showed off her cleavage.

Shit, just thinking about it was getting his dick hard. She was every school boy's wet dream. Tom realised, as he'd moved from being a boy into manhood that she was enticing him. He was tall, muscular from all the gardening jobs he did, had great hair that flopped into his dark brown eyes, and had long dark lashes and plump, full lips that he'd pleasured quite a few girls with - she wanted him, he was sure and he would be more than up for the job. He hadn't had sex yet, but he was sure that he'd watched enough porn, listened to enough girls moaning at his touch, to know that he could easily pleasure Mrs Brady, should the opportunity arise.

"Fuuuck," he groaned, adjusting his jeans.

Mrs Brady had opened the door and was wearing the tiniest pair of cut-off shorts he'd ever seen and a tiny bikini top that barely covered her nipples.

"You okay, Tom?" she asked, licking her lips.

Oh yeah, she was fucking magnificent.

"Sorry, Mrs Brady," he replied, thrusting his backpack in front of his crotch. "Just remembered something I should have done."

"Oh, do you need to go home?"

Tom shook his head vehemently. "No. No. Not at all. It's fine."

"Okay, well come in then." Mrs Brady stood to one

side and ushered Tom in.

She'd barely given him enough room, and as he passed, Tom's arm brushed against her breast. Tom bit down on his lip, worried that he might blow his load. Although, if he didn't he might have to consider going to the bathroom and wanking off because he wasn't sure he could push a lawn mower with a dick as hard as granite. It'd be too fucking painful.

"Before you do the lawn, can you help me with something else?" Mrs Brady asked.

Tom stopped and looked over his shoulder. "Sure, Mrs Brady. What can I help you with?" He threw her his best smile. The one that usually got the girls at college to open their blouses, or pull up their skirts for him.

Tom Davies was nothing if not confident. He was an almost eighteen-year old virgin, but he knew how to work a woman up and he was sure that included those a decade older than him. The only reason he hadn't lost his virginity yet was because up until going to college, his parents hadn't liked him going out, so he'd had no real interest in girls, he hadn't really had any contact with them. Plus, if he was being honest, he'd been a little bit skinny and gangly. But, after a summer of mowing lawns and weeding flowerbeds, he'd filled out and grown into his looks and realised that he had a natural charm with the opposite sex. On his first day at college, when he'd got talking to Jake Hughes who'd gone to the same school as him, he was amazed at the number of admiring glances that he'd got from girls. That along with being part of the band with Jake, Luke Mahoney and Antony Ballard, or Skins as he liked to be known, meant that he was now popular with girls. The only problem was the girls at their college were playing hard to get and a quick orgasm with his tongue or fingers were about as far as they were willing to let him go - either that or Jake, Luke or Skins had already had them, and he didn't fancy sloppy seconds, or thirds in a couple of cases - not for his first time. So, he'd been a little discerning and decided that his first time would be epic and not him blowing his load after a couple of thrusts into some pretty college girl. No, Tom Davies decided almost a month ago that Mrs Brady would be the one to show him exactly what to do. All he had to do was charm her, and hope that the skimpy clothes, swaying hips and brushing of her tits against him wasn't all just her teasing a teenage boy. He didn't think so because she'd been doing it for months now, and Tom had waited until he could be sure. Well the tiny bikini top made him think she was more than fucking ready. Her next sentence just proved it.

"I need some help with a light bulb in the bedroom. Mr Brady is away on business for a week and I'm pretty desperate."

Yep, she was ready.

Without any thought of whether what he was about to do was right, wrong or even legal, he placed his backpack and guitar case under the stairs.

"Lead the way."

Mrs Brady smiled and started up the stairs, with that extra sway in her hips that Tom loved so much.

Almost an hour later and the lawn hadn't been mowed and nor had the lightbulb been changed. When they'd entered the bedroom, she'd brushed against him and Tom had felt how hard her nipples were against her bikini top. Briefly thinking he could be about to get himself into some big trouble, and ignoring that thought, he placed an arm around her waist and pulled her against his chest.

"Tom," she'd gasped. "What are you doing?"

Looking down at her, Tom licked his lips, considered apologising and running out and then captured her mouth in his. He kept kissing her, while his fingers whispered over the bare skin of her waist and back, and finally threaded into her hair, wrapping it around his hand. With his dick harder than he'd ever thought possible, Tom moved a hand to the button of her shorts and popped it open.

"Say no now Mrs Brady, if this isn't what you want."

Mrs Brady moaned and pushed her hips forward. "I need your fingers inside me now, Tom."

Never one to disappoint a lady, Tom did as she

asked and slowly lowered her zipper before pushing his hand inside her knickers. With two fingers and his thumb he brought her to orgasm, swallowing her cries into his mouth as he continued to kiss her.

"Your turn."

Still panting, Mrs Brady dropped to her knees and undid Tom's jeans and pulled them down with his boxers, allowing his erection to spring free.

"Fuck me," she whispered. "You're going to fuck me with that amazing thing, but first I'm going to give you the best blow job you will ever have."

Tom dropped his head back and groaned as her wet lips engorged him. She pumped him while her tongue swirled around his head, and then she pulled her mouth away slowly. Moaning, she stuck out her tongue and licked up and down Tom's shaft, while her fingers dug into his arse cheeks. Finally, she closed her mouth around him again and pumped him in time with her head movements. Tom gripped the back of Mrs Brady's head, holding her in place while his hips relaxed into her rhythm. As the pressure grew, Tom felt the tingle start as every part of his body felt as though it was electrified.

"Mrs Brady," he groaned. "I'm close."

She looked up at him through her lashes and smiled around his cock, pulling just a little bit harder. That was all it took to send Tom over the edge and he came cursing and thanking god all at the same time.

"Fuuuuck. Oh my God. Fuuuck."

Pushing on Mrs Brady's head, making sure she milked him dry, Tom panted and wondered whether he would ever feel as amazing as that ever again. Five minutes later he had his answer. Mrs Brady was on the bed, stark-naked, her legs open and touching herself.

"Come on Tom," she called. "I need you."

Throwing his Converse and clothes to one side, Tom joined her on the bed. He wanted to take it slow, not wanting to come across as the eager little virgin, but she was so fucking beautiful he didn't think he could. Plus, he had promised Luke he wouldn't be late, so with the time it took to get to Luke's house, Tom reckoned he had just over half an hour to make Mrs Brady scream his name. Seeing as it was his first time, he also reckoned he could probably get her to do that twice, one way or another.

Scooting down to the bottom of the bed, Tom recalled some of the things he'd seen on the porn he'd watched. He wasn't sure he had the expertise for a lot of it, but he'd at least got some idea of what he needed to do. Pushing her legs open wider, Tom kissed up the inside of her thigh, first on one side and then the other, all while Mrs Brady continued to touch herself. When her breathing changed, Tom pushed her fingers away and replaced them with his mouth. Sucking and licking until her back arched from the bed.

"Don't come yet," he murmured, trying to sound

more confident than he felt.

Reaching down for his jeans, he shook out a condom from his back pocket. The same one he'd carried with him for the last month, since he'd decided Mrs Brady would be the one. Ripping open the packet, Tom kneeled between Mrs Brady's legs and rolled the condom on, glad that he'd been practising with the bananas that his dad liked to take to work in his packed lunch.

"You ready for me, Mrs Brady?" he asked, coughing to hide the quiver in his voice.

"Oh God, yes," she breathed out, pinching her nipples.

Tom would have liked to think the sex had been as good as the blow job, but he hadn't lasted long, despite already coming only ten minutes before. It had only taken a few thrusts until he was groaning out his release. As he did, Mrs Brady bought herself to climax, slipping a hand between them, and as she also came her inner walls gripped his dick, sending the sensation to another level for Tom.

"Shit," Tom groaned, rolling off her. "That was a bit quick, sorry about that."

"Don't be sorry, Tom," she said breathily. "It was great. I think the next time will be much better."

Tom turned his head and looked at her with wide eyes. "What you want to do this again, next time I come to mow your lawn?"

"No Tom," she said with a tinkle of laughter.

"Today is a one-time only deal. We're actually moving away, my husband has got a promotion to another bank in Birmingham."

Tom felt a little twinge in his chest, but it was only momentary. Mrs Brady was amazing, and sexy as fuck, but she was just that - a Mrs. She was married and Tom did not need that shit. He had his whole life ahead of him. He'd always remember her, but just as a happy memory.

"So, you think you can go again?" Mrs Brady asked, taking hold of Tom's dick.

He looked down on it, and as she rubbed the end of it with her thumb, it got hard all over again.

"Yeah, but I don't have another condom."

"Don't you worry about that, I have plenty. So, we going one more round?"

Tom nodded and this time enjoyed the sight of Mrs Brady's fabulous tits jiggling up and down while she went on top and rode him with all the experience of an older woman.

CHAPTER 16

♥

PRESENT DAY

"You dirty dog," Skins said amidst the laughter. "You never said that night."

"She asked me to keep it a secret. I just figured once she moved away, and a few years passed it didn't matter that I told you."

"You never saw her again?" Jake asked.

Tom shook his head. "Nope. The house went on the market the following week, but they moved before it was sold."

"What about the rest of your customers. Any of

them receive the Tom Davies special treatment." Luke shook his head, still unable to believe Tom hadn't told them until years later. If he'd shagged an older woman when he was eighteen, he'd have told anyone that would listen.

"No, they were all too old. Although, there was the granddaughter of Mr and Mrs Taylor. She was staying for the summer and so by the last couple of weeks of her stay we were at it like rabbits. The Taylor's had the best kept garden in town."

"Oh yeah, I remember her," Jake cried. "You brought her to band practice one night, didn't you? Pretty girl, long blonde hair."

Tom nodded and smiled. He'd really liked Kelly, but she lived in Bristol, so that was never going to be anything more than a summer fling.

"No one ever found out, her husband never suspected?" Skins asked of Mrs Brady.

"Nope, not that I know of. Her old neighbour told me about a year later that she was having a baby, so I'm assuming it was her husband's."

"And she was curvy like your Gibson?"

"Yeah, she was all woman. Curves, tits and long legs. Pretty perfect for my first time."

"Christ, mine was a disaster," Luke chipped in. "I think I only thrust twice and came like a fucking rocket."

"Shit," Jake said. "The great Luke Mahoney admitting he isn't very good at something."

"Hey, I never said I wasn't any good. My wife is perfectly happy thank you. I just said the first time was shit. I wasn't born an expert, I had to learn. Look at the Karate Kid." He winked at Jake and slapped his back.

"Whatever, you still admitted you were shit once and that's the thing I'll remember most about today."

"Fuck off, Jake," Luke grumbled, but with a smile on his face.

"And was it the best blow job you've ever had?" Skins asked.

"No, no, no, no, no!" Jake held his hands up. "He's married to my sister, I do not want to know."

"Yeah but we do," Luke said. "So?"

"At the time, yeah. Probably up until I was about twenty-five and I had that fling with Kitten the stripper from Vegas."

"A stripper called Kitten has given you the best blow job ever? Okay interesting," Skins said. "You obviously have high standards."

"Never said that." Tom shook his head. "Let's say that both Mrs Brady and Kitten are in the top six. Also, let's say that the other four in the top six have been in the last three years, so what does that tell you? In fact, the one that was probably the best was just last night."

"Fuck, I damn well knew it." Jake stamped his foot and groaned. "It's my sister dude."

"You fucking asked!"

"*I* didn't," Jake protested. He pointed at Luke. "*He* did. You could have waited until I left the room."

"Sorry buddy," Tom said, but his laughter kind of proved he wasn't sorry at all.

"Ugh, it's just nasty."

"Oh, and it's not nasty me thinking about you and my cousin," Luke replied. "Cause, that kills me too. Of all the men in the world, I can't believe she chose you."

Jake turned on him, his mouth open with a gasp.

"How can you say that? You know we were made for each other."

Luke shrugged. "Ah, I'm not so sure. I definitely think that there was someone more suitable out there. You just happened to come along at the right time."

Luke ducked as Jake's hand shot out towards him.

"Take that back, fucker."

Luke started to laugh as Jake's lips pouted.

"Ah, whatever. You make her happy so I suppose I can't complain." He leaned in and kissed Jake's forehead. "I love ya buddy."

Jake swiped at his head with the back of his hand. "Don't think you can get around me with kisses, Luke. I'm not that easy."

"I think you'll find you are," Skins laughed out. "What about that DJ when we went on her breakfast show? I believe we were only five minutes into the interview, before you let her rub you one out with her foot under the desk."

"Fuck yeah," Tom exclaimed. "Neither him nor she faltered. She kept asking questions and playing records as though nothing was going on."

"Only until he came," Luke added. "Don't you remember he was halfway through an answer about where we'd recorded the album and suddenly shouted 'hell yeah'."

They all burst out laughing, remembering how Jake had needed to tie his jacket around his waist to hide the wet patch on his jeans.

"To be fair to me," Jake said as their laughter subsided. "I had woken up late and hadn't had time to have a wank in the shower. So, I was primed and ready to go for her. She didn't have to try very hard."

"Yeah, but five minutes, dude," Skins grumbled. "That's quick even by your standards."

"We had been introduced ten minutes before that," Tom replied. "So, I guess it's officially fifteen minutes. Still impressive, Jake."

He high-fived Jake, who grinned mischievously at him.

"All change now though," Luke sighed. "We're all happily married with families. Who'd have thought it?"

"Shit, Luke. You sound like some old grandad. You're meant to be the 'Sex God of Rock'," Tom said grumpily.

"I am," Luke protested.

"Yeah," Skins added. "Just the 'Sex God of Rock'

that pisses himself and needs a little blue pill to get it up."

"Ha-ha, very funny. We all know that it's not me that needs a little blue pill. Isn't that right, Antony?"

Tom and Jake swivelled to face Skins, both with huge ass grins on their faces.

"It was one fucking time," Skins protested, poking Luke in the shoulder. "You promised you wouldn't say anything."

Luke shrugged. "Yeah well, I lied."

"Oh, fuck me, this is the best news ever." Jake sat down on one of the couches, dragging Skins down next to him. "Go on, tell us. You might as well now."

CHAPTER 17

♥

5 YEARS EARLIER

"Seriously, Luke this is not fucking funny." Skins let out a moan as he looked down at his crotch. His dick was as hard as concrete and wasn't about to go down anytime soon.

Luke bit on his top lip, trying to stem the laughter for two reasons. One, he knew Skins could pack a punch, and two, Martha was in the next room watching TV and he did not want her seeing Skins hard on. It was fucking obscene.

"So, how many pills did you take exactly?"

"Just the one, but it must be some strong shit because this fucker has been like this for over an hour." Skins scrubbed a hand over his bald head and let out a withering sigh. "What the fuck am I going to do?"

Luke inclined his head to one side – sizing up the problem – and though it pained him, he had to admit his friend was extremely well blessed. Obviously, they'd seen each other naked over the years, but up close and personal, Skins' hard on was something to behold, even underneath his clothes.

"Why the fuck are you studying it?" Skins blasted. "Stop looking and think of something."

"Me looking at it hasn't helped it wither then?" Luke asked. "Cause, I know if you, Tom or Jake were looking at my junk that fucker would shrivel faster than a slug with salt on it."

"Well mine hasn't." Skins pointed down at the offending area. "Obviously."

"Do you think maybe you could be bisexual?" Before he even had time to shout out that it was a joke, he felt the punch to his bicep. "Okay, okay," he said laughing and rubbing at his arm. "Evidently not."

"No, now just damn well help me."

"What am I supposed to do? Ugh, you don't want me to wank you off, do you?"

"No!" Skins cried. "I don't, you stupid toss pot."

"Okay, keep your voice down. Martha's in the next

room. Do you want her to come out here to find out what's going on?" Luke moved over to his study door and clicked it shut.

"Why the hell was the door open in the first place?" Skins shook his head and thrust his hands to his hips.

"Because I don't feel comfortable in a room with that," Luke said pointing at Skins erection, "with the door closed. If anyone came in they'd think totally the wrong thing."

Luke moved past Skins and went to sit down at his desk, turning on his laptop.

"What are you doing?" Skins asked impatiently.

"*Googling* it. It has an answer for everything."

Skins lowered himself gingerly into the chair on the opposite side of the desk to Luke, and waited with a pained expression on his face.

"Wow, who knew that there were so many products on the market. Why didn't you tell me you had erectile dysfunction? I would have helped."

Luke grinned at Skins, enjoying his anxiety and wishing that Tom and Jake were there to see it. Other than when he'd been an addict, Skins was always in tight control. He never messed up and never put himself in a position for the rest of them to take the piss out of him-so this was comedy gold.

"Don't you dare tell the other two," Skins snapped correctly reading the grin on Luke's face. "And I don't fucking have erectile dysfunction."

"So, why'd you take it then?" Luke watched him

with narrowed eyes. "And as an addict, should you really be taking drugs of any kind-even if it is to get your dick hard?"

"I thought it was a *'Smint'*," Skins groaned. "I'd sneaked outside for a cigarette, and heard Stace coming, and was searching my jacket pocket for gum-I've always got fucking gum, but oh no, not today. Today I found a *mint* that sent my dick rock hard."

Luke let out a huge belly laugh as he watched his friend wriggle awkwardly and adjust the crotch of his jeans.

"This isn't funny, Luke."

"Yeah it kinda is," Luke said breathlessly as he wiped at his eyes.

"Whatever, just try and find me a solution."

Skins petulantly shoved his chair back and lifted his leg to cross it. When the discomfort hit him, he groaned and stretched both his legs out in front of him instead. This caused another chuckle from Luke.

"Why were you smoking, anyway?" he asked. "You haven't smoked in almost six years."

Skins shrugged. "Don't know, just fancied one. I keep a packet in my office, just in case. Probably had the same packet for five years, that's how often I smoke. Probably had three in that six years."

"More worryingly, is who the fuck put drugs in the pocket of an addict?" Luke's face was now serious, as he considered the consequences.

"No idea. It had to be somewhere I had my jacket

on, so probably a party, or even an interview. I don't care as long as it wears off soon."

Luke continued looking at his screen and then sighed with relief. "Okay, looks like you can't get addicted, unless of course you really need it. Which you don't...do you?"

"No, you fucker, I don't. I told you I thought it was a damn mint. Now I'm in trouble for smoking, because Stace could smell it on me, *and* she thinks I'm being childish and have stormed off in a mood because she kicked off about it."

Luke's lips twitched into a small smile as he read the information on screen. "So, as you don't need it, it's unlikely you'll get addicted. The only high you get from is the multiple orgasms, because your dick will stay harder for longer."

"How long? Because I've got to be honest with you Luke, I can't hide away from my wife for much longer."

"Why didn't you just tell her, you idiot?" Luke sat back in his chair, linking his hands behind his head, and stretching his legs out.

"Because like you, she'll panic that I'm going to get addicted. We don't have so much as an antiseptic throat sweet in the house, she's so fucking worried."

Luke's smile fell from his face. "Seriously?"

"Yeah," Skins sighed. "She's petrified that I'll take something in all innocence that will set me off on that shitty trail of addiction again. Even Ethan's '*Calpol*' is locked in her bedside drawer.

"Has it always been like this?" Luke asked, concern etched on his handsome features.

Skins shook his head. "Nope, just since we've had Ethan. I think she's worried that if I do get ill again, she won't be able to look after me and him, so she's doing what she can to make sure it never happens."

"Skins man, that's not right. She needs to see someone, a therapist maybe. I can put you in touch with who I used for my stage fright."

"Yeah maybe. She's cool, most of the time, you know what she's like - more chilled out than anyone I know. It's just anything to do with drugs, of any kind, freaks her out."

"That's understandable," Luke replied sitting forwards. "But she has to trust you."

He totally understood Stacey's worry, he worried regularly about his best friend relapsing, but it sounded as though Stacey was worried to the point of hysteria. That in the long term would not be good for her, or her relationship with Skins.

"She does trust me," Skins replied. "She knows I'm not going to go out and score. No, her worry is that even the most innocuous pain killer will have something in it that gets me hooked. And to be honest, I agree. I don't want to take anything unless I really have to. But, she does need to lighten up and trust that I stick to it. So, you see, telling her I've just taken a drug that makes my dick hard, would not be helpful."

Skins rubbed a hand over his head and muttered a curse. He'd put Stacey through so much heartache when he'd been using, so he totally understood her anxiety, but Luke was right. Stacey needed to get some help – they both did – to get some coping mechanisms to avoid it taking over their lives to the point where they were crippled with stress.

Luke nodded. "Okay," he said pushing up from his chair. "There's only one thing for it."

"What's that?"

"You have to go upstairs to the bathroom and slap the monkey. That's all there is to it."

"WHAT?" Skins got up from his chair and leaned over the desk towards Luke. "No fucking way. I'm not going upstairs to your bathroom, with your kid asleep down the landing, and wanking off. Nope, not happening."

He started to pace up and down the room, muttering to himself and rubbing a hand over his shaved head.

"Buddy, it's either that or go home and tell Stace that you need to have sex with her for the next three hours."

"Three hours? That's really how long I need to fucking masturbate for?"

"No way, you're not fucking thrashing your dick in my bathroom for three hours. No, go and rub a couple out and then go home and treat Stace to the night of her life."

"I should just go home then. Why do I need to go upstairs?" Skins face was full of discomfort and it wasn't just from the ache in his boxers. The thought of doing that in Luke and Martha's house made him feel defiled-just not enough to make his dick shrink in his pants.

"If you can explain to Stacey why you need to keep going for up to three hours, or that she's going to have to help you out for a while, then go for it. At least if you visit my bathroom you might only have to only do it a couple of times."

"Not like it'd be a chore," Skins said with a glint in his eye. He loved his wife, and she was the sexiest damn woman on the planet. Maybe this wasn't such a bad thing-but he knew Stace and after two orgasms she'd be done and ready to sleep. That made him smile, the fact that he could sex his wife into oblivion. That was how it always was, he knew no other way to love her but hard and intense-no, twice and she'd be asleep and he'd be left with the same problem.

"This is not right," Skins muttered as he stormed out of the room.

When he slipped back into Luke's office, Skins knew that his face was burning red. He couldn't be anymore ashamed.

"This is a fucking nightmare," he groaned. "I can't believe it."

"Well, did it help?" Luke asked, chewing the inside of his cheek.

"Oh, it's peachy. And the cherry on my fucking cake, was bumping into your mamma on her way to her room."

Luke didn't know whether to laugh or cry for his friend-and his mother for that matter. "Did she see that?" he asked, pointing at the still impressive bulge in Skins' jeans.

"I held my hands in front of it. She probably thinks I've pissed myself and didn't want her to see."

Luke couldn't help but laugh, but quickly stopped when he saw the look of rage on his friend's face.

"Sorry, buddy. So, um , how many did you...you know...how many times did you-"

"Three, okay. Now shut the fuck up. I'm going home to make love to my wife."

"Let's hope she hasn't got a headache."

"Very fucking funny, Luke."

Skins edged his way to the door, adjusting himself as he did so. "And don't you dare tell Tom or Jake," he snapped, with his hand on the handle.

"I won't," Luke said holding his hands up. "I swear."

Skins pulled the door open and stepped into the hallway.

"Oh hi, Skins."

Skins rolled his eyes and inhaled deeply, before looking over his shoulder towards the owner of the voice. "Hey Martha, how are you doing, babe?"

"Good thanks, you okay?"

"Fine. Yep."

"Stace and Ethan?"

"Yep, they're good too." He gave Martha a brief smile and then glanced at Luke, silently begging him for help.

"Skins is just going, baby," Luke said. "He's got stuff to do."

"Yes," Martha replied. "It's *hard* when you've got a family isn't it?"

Skins gaze moved back to her, sure she'd just emphasised the word 'hard'.

"Yep, it is," he replied, hoping he'd imagined it.

"Hmm, Stace and I were only talking yesterday, about how *hard* it is. Luckily though we're not married to *wankers* like some people, which is a great *relief*."

Skins whipped around, forgetting about the bulge in his trousers. As he did, Martha's eyes lowered and she burst into laughter.

"You fucker." Skins rounded on Luke, pointing a finger in his face. "You promised."

"I promised not to tell Jake or Tom, you didn't mention Martha."

"I thought you'd understand that, you knob head."

"Oh, I'm sorry, Skins," Martha gasped, holding her sides. "It's just so funny."

Skins didn't answer, but stormed down the

hallway, double flipping his friends the bird over his shoulders.

"Not again," Stacey groaned. "I'm knackered, my fanny is sore and my biceps feel as though I've been lifting weights for hours."

"How's your jaw feeling?" Skins asked. "Is that okay?"

The pillow bashed against his dick did nothing whatsoever to diminish its hardness, so for the second time that night, Skins found himself rubbing a couple out in the bathroom.

CHAPTER 18

♥

PRESENT DAY

"So, Luke, how would you sum up the last twenty-five years that you've been together?"

After almost six hours, the interview was finally ending and while it had been a long day, the band had enjoyed it. As promised, Mike hadn't referred to any unwanted subjects but had asked interesting questions that delved deep into the psyche of them as a band and individuals – drawing out detail that no one had ever got from them before.

Leaning back in his chair and steepling his fingers

under his chin, Mike waited for Luke's reply.

Luke finally blew out a breath and shook his head. "God, that's difficult. Twenty-five years as a band is a lot of memories to wrap up in one sentence."

"We have the damn photographs to prove that," Jake said, nodding his head at the piles of pictures spread across the table.

"Some of which should never have seen the light of day," Tom quipped, holding up a photograph of Jake in a woman's corset and high heels.

They all laughed as Luke turned back to Mike. "I guess to sum up, I'd say it's been a fucking blast. These guys, well they're not just my band members, they're my brothers too. We're a family, always have been and always will be. No matter what life throws at us, we stick together because we love each other and I can't think of any other people that I'd rather have done this with. To be honest, if just one of the personnel had been different, I don't think it would have worked. We are the best rock band in the world because it's *us*-this four people here are who make Dirty Riches the best there has ever been."

Mike reached for his recorder and pressed a button. "That's it guys. All done."

"Phew," Skins, replied. "That actually wasn't as bad as I expected. Thanks, Mike."

"My pleasure. I think we got some really good stuff, and I can't wait for you to read it."

"As long as you remember to put in the bit about

Jake and the cow." Tom grinned as Jake flipped a hand at him.

"I don't think Jake would allow that, would you?" Mike asked on a laugh.

"Too fucking right. It was bad enough he used it in his best man's speech at my wedding. I don't want the whole world knowing about it."

They all began to laugh, including Jake. As Mike started to pack away his notebook and recorder, a knock came at the door and it was slowly opened.

Martha's head appeared around it.

"Hey baby," Luke said, a huge smile enveloping his face.

"We're not too early, are we?" she asked, moving into the room, her hands resting on her pregnant belly. "I've got the whole gang with me."

Mike shook his head and turned to the photographer, who had been quietly snapping away during the interview.

"Sam, you ready?"

"Sure am. Just need to set up another light, but am thinking over on the stage would be good."

Mike had had the idea to conduct the interview where it had all begun for the band – the college social club where they'd played their first gig.

"Get them all in then, baby."

Martha disappeared, momentarily, but was soon back with the rest of the Dirty Riches family in tow. Mike felt that pictures of the wives and children would be a good addition to the piece, and the band had all agreed – while music was still important to them, their families were their lives.

Sam, the photographer, assembled everyone on the stage and threw a few inflatable balls on with them, as well as handing out some bottles of bubbles, telling them to have fun. And so they did - Martha and Amber blew bubbles for Rafa, Jackson and Hendrix, Stacey kicked the inflatable balls around with Rocco and Ethan, while Abbie held Hettie to her hip as she danced around with Eliza and Gigi. There was a lot of laughter and huge smiles of happiness from all of them.

"Fuck, we're lucky," Luke said as he and the rest of the band lined up to watch. "That's my life, up there on that stage and I thank God every fucking day for them."

"Tell me about it," Jake sighed. "The music is great, but without *them* it would be nothing. Did I tell you that Eliza wants to be in a band, when she grows up?"

"Tell her to be the drummer," Skins replied. "Because we all know-"

"Yeah, we know," Tom cut in. "The drummer *keeps* the beat. Shit, play another record."

Skins flipped Tom the bird and turned to Jake. "So, go on, she wants to be in a band?"

"Yeah, she has a name for it and has already said she wants to play guitar, like her daddy."

"What...badly?"

Without even looking at him, Jake scuffed Tom around the back of the head.

"As I was saying," Jake continued. "She wants to play guitar and wants to call her band, Snake Bandit."

Luke whistled. "Wow, cool name. How the hell did she come up with that?"

"'Cause she's a fucking cool kid." Jake frowned as though Luke had just said *the* most, nonsensical sentence ever.

"At least she's put her brain to good use. I know they're only young, but Rocco worries me," Luke groaned as he looked over to the stage where his son was smoothing back his hair.

"Why, because he's so like you?" Skins said with a grin. "I mean look at him, he's too damn suave to be an eight-year-old kid."

"He's going to be a damn handful, I know that much," Luke sighed. "He told me that when he grows up he wants to kiss girls - lots of them."

"Like father like son."

Luke glared at Tom. "Well, let's just hope that Hettie isn't one of those girls."

Tom blanched and shook his head. "Oh no, she's not leaving the house until she's at least thirty, and even then, she'll be chaperoned. We've been those dick pieces that fuck and run, and I'm not risking my little girl meeting anyone like we were."

"Well my boy has already started," Skins said.

"He's got a girlfriend at school."

"He's only just ten, what the fuck?" Jake asked, aghast.

"Oh, don't worry," Skins replied, shaking his head. "He's dumping her on Monday, because, and I quote 'she's too needy'. Plus, a new girl has started, and she's much prettier, apparently."

"That's it," Tom cried. "Hettie isn't going out until she's forty-years of age, thirty is far too young."

As they all started to laugh, their individual gazes went over to the stage where their wives and children were now all dancing and singing along to the Dirty Riches hit, 'Bring it on'. Each band member felt their hearts swell as they looked on and recalled how they'd manage to get to such a good place in their lives.

"Well," Luke finally spoke. "I think we can safely say we are the luckiest men alive."

"Totally agree," Tom replied.

"Yep, I feel like my balls are platinum, never mind golden." Jake nodded towards the stage.

"Do we have to talk about your balls, again?" Skins asked. "Every conversation either gets around to your balls, your dick or even your fucking ass."

"Yeah, but what a tight, pert ass it is," Jake said as he turned around and rubbed his backside against Skins' groin. "Go on admit it, you want it."

"Fuck off!" Skins pushed Jake away.

"What if I wore a sparkly red thong, would that do

it for you-?"

As Skins chased Jake around the room, everyone stopped to watch and laugh, grateful for everything and looking forward to the next twenty-five years.

The End...for now

MORE BOOKS BY
NIKKI ASHTON

Guess Who I Pulled Last Night?
No Bra Required
Get Your Kit Off
Rock Stars Don't Like Big Knickers

All books are standalone stories, with 'guest'
appearances from characters in the previous book

Please visit Nikki's Facebook page Nikki Ashton's
Books for news, snippets and pictures

You can also follow Nikki on Twitter @nikkerash

Printed by Amazon Italia Logistica S.r.l.
Torrazza Piemonte (TO), Italy

11532763R00089